SECTIONS OF AN ORANGE

ACKNOWLEDGEMENTS OF PREVIOUS PUBLICATION:

"Time and Tide" in *Our Caribbean: a gathering of lesbian and gay writing from the Antilles*
"On The Side", "Marjory's Meal" and "Just Now" in *Calabash, A Journal of Caribbean Arts and Letters*
"Sections of an Orange" in *African American Review*
"Into My Parlor" in *African Voices*

SECTIONS OF AN ORANGE

AND OTHER STORIES

ANTON NIMBLETT

PEEPAL TREE

First published in Great Britain in 2009
Peepal Tree Press Ltd
17 King's Avenue
Leeds LS6 1QS
England

ISBN13: 9781845230746

 Peepal Tree gratefully acknowledges Arts Council support

CONTENTS

Visiting Soldiers   7

Into My Parlour   30

On the Side   36

Time and Tide   49

Just Now   59

Marjory's Meal   75

How Far, How Long   88

Sections of an Orange   99

Ring Games   113

Mr. Parker's Behaviour   127

One, Two, Three – Push   133

For Deryck, For Vanessa
for unimagined possibility...

VISITING SOLDIERS

Evangeline Leonard has been walking around with her son's ashes for weeks. The sleek urn is at the bottom of the leather tote that she has carried every day for years – winter or summer, work or play. Sometimes there's an extra pair of shoes in the bag, sometimes a packed lunch, always her *Daily Word* magazine. Comfortable shoes because Eva likes to dress up, but respects her corns and bunions. A packed lunch because Eva would rather spend money on nice heels than on six-dollar sandwiches.

The ashes of her only son Roderick rest beneath a copy of the New Testament. No one's noticed. Not co-workers, not friends and not family – all who worried, at first, that Eva would never be herself again after the loss of her son. But Eva has surprised them all, really, from the time that the news was delivered.

Her younger sister Naomi answered the door, saw the soldiers in dress greens and knew right away – from the movies, from TV, from the nightmares that fret every family with a relative in combat. Bad news.

Naomi sat next to Eva in the living room while an officer delivered his speech – rehearsed but compassionate, like an accomplished actor performing a monologue for the nth time. The other officer sat quiet, holding an oppressively official-looking envelope.

Naomi wasn't sure how Eva would react. There were two possibilities. She pictured her sister wailing, a channel for all the black women who have cried before her: girlfriends who wailed for first-loves shot down a block from home by a gang-banger's stray bullet or by a cop's panic; wives who bawled for husbands lost in Vietnam or Korea; mothers who howled for sons as overseers striped bare black backs. Naomi knew that Eva had those timeworn wails in her. Long, loud cries lifted up to God.

More likely though, Eva would have a different fire in her eyes, hurling steely ire at these bearers of bad news, throwing quiet curse words like quick jabbing fists. Words Eva hadn't used in the years since she'd been saved, but words that she could still string together with a wharf woman's precision. Eva had defended Naomi throughout childhood with this skill – never a bruised knuckle – just the mouth that the headmistress said "surely didn't come from any angel". The curses would be so specific to a distant time and place that the men might not understand the Trinidadian parlance. But the inflections, the anger would be unmistakable.

Naomi waited, unsure about which reaction would be easier to manage or even which would be the healthier response for her sister.

Instead, when the senior officer finished his speech, there was only silence. Not a weighty silence that simmered with loudness yet to come. No, Eva was calm. The officers were controlled. Naomi was still.

"Well, you gentlemen look like you had a long day," Eva said after a while. "You must have a little something to eat with me."

The younger officer started to reply – another prepared speech.

"Just a li'l something with me. Please. Besides, Naomi now-now finish making a nice pot of *pelau*," Eva said. "And watch at Naomi size, yuh see for yuhself that she could cook good."

Naomi almost smiled at the backhanded compliment lobbed her way.

The senior officer nodded – an affirmative to Eva, an instruction for his partner.

The four ate together. Small servings. Little talk. A 'thank you'. A fork clinked light against a plate. Four pairs of eyes alternated between focusing on the food, and darting about the room. When, eventually, Naomi looked over to her sister, about to ask if she was ok, she found Eva staring at the younger man. She couldn't decipher the look on her face, but Naomi could see that this was no time for her question.

Eva had been staring at the junior officer long before Naomi noticed. The senior officer had noticed, making him regret his decision to break regulations. His concern grew that this might turn out even worse than he'd imagined – not that these visits could ever go well.

The junior officer had met eyes with Eva once, and thereafter kept his gaze on his own hand as it guided forkfuls of rice to his mouth, trying to suggest he was unaware of Eva's gaze.

Corporal Parks's apparent unawareness – Eva had checked his name-tag – made her stare all the more. He looked about the same age as Roderick. But then, young men in military uniforms all looked the same age: boys too-young to be at war, cleverly costumed to look like grown men. But, more than how young Corporal Parks looked, there was something in his manner that suggested Roderick. Perhaps the way he angled his neck, the fact that though he was the quietest one in the room, he had the strongest presence. He was taller and thinner than Roderick, he was white, but somehow he was sitting in Eva's living room with her, like Roderick often had. Like Roderick never would again.

Despite the senior officer's concerns, despite the junior officer's crafted unawareness, despite Naomi's predictions, the official visit ended quietly. Eva excused herself, said good night. The soldiers left paperwork and contact information with Naomi, and she walked them out. Afterwards, she found Eva in her bedroom, not sprawled across the bed or beating fists against the wall, but on the phone.

"They just leave," she was saying. "Yes, yes they sure that is Roderick. He gone."

The next days brought more surprises for Naomi, and for Eva's other family and friends. Each had different explanations for Eva's strong facade – "She in shock," "Give her time," "Yuh know she's a good Christian woman, she have the strength of The Lord" – but no one could explain her decisions.

First, Eva got up and got dressed for work the morning after the soldiers visited. She only agreed to stay home after Naomi insisted, pointing out there were arrangements to be made and company to be expected.

Then, when Eva's eldest sister, Stella, came over with her family, Eva latched on to Stella's grandson. After she'd spent a few minutes answering the questions that she would have to answer over and over in the next days, questions-and-answers that would become a litany, Eva pulled Chad away and sat with him at the computer. Chad was fifteen. Eva had never used the computer, not once. It sat in the far corner of the living room collecting dust like a cheap knickknack, bothered only on the occasions when Naomi turned it on to play solitaire. Eva had long maintained, "Not me and that, nah, I too old for computer and dem thing so." Eva was only fifty-eight the first time she said this, but as her brother-in-law was quick to observe, women from the West Indies are ever ready to sing the too-old-blues. Eva's brother-in-law, Stella's husband, was from Barbados, but he loved all things American.

Too-old Eva spent the evening working at the PC with Chad. Stella, Naomi and the rest, let her be. They honoured the wide berth, granted by custom, to the bereaved – granted especially to the one with the most right to grieve: the young widow, the octogenarian widower who has been part of a couple for three quarter of his life, the mother of a fallen soldier.

Chad, for his part, was glad to be helping his aunt. Yes, he was more sensitive, more empathetic than boys his age tend to be, but he was also glad to have his computer skills appreciated. At home he was used to being ridiculed for his hobby, accustomed to his grandfather's comments about "life passing by while you sit in front of that blasted blinking screen." If Chad had been bolder, he'd have voiced what he thought when he heard this nagging: *Yes Granddad, it's called electricity, not like when you were my age.* But now here was Auntie Eva, of all people, asking him questions and taking instructions on software and file folders and the internet. The computer was kind of an old clunker and Aunt Eva didn't have any experience at all, but he was patient and clear, and she was paying attention. She was learning.

The entire night passed like that. Naomi took the phone calls and Stella and her husband sat with the neighbours who came by. When her sister's family was halfway out of the door, Eva asked if Chad could come by after school the next day to continue the lesson. In the surprised pause that followed her request, Eva said, "I'll pay the boy for lessons. I know children these days like a little bit of change in they pocket." And before either Chad or his grandparents could respond, Eva added, "Besides, I know that expert tutors don't come for free." Chad puffed up a bit at his new title and stole a look at his grandfather.

Eva's offer to pay underscored her resolve, though it didn't come to an exchange of money when Chad returned the next day. Eva followed an instinct that led her to the machine that had been Roderick's and to his address book on the hard drive. Eva, with Chad's help, sent emails to Roderick's friends – some from high school, some from his year after graduation when he worked at Radio Shack in the mall. She wouldn't have been able to contact those old friends without the computer, or without Chad.

With the announcement of the death and details of the funeral went an instruction to wear casual clothing, no uniforms. Eva directed the funeral home to say the same thing when giving any information out over the phone. Naomi and Stella, especially, were drilled to ensure that they followed the 'no uniform' script too.

Naomi tried to argue. "Roderick's friends from the service will want to come and..."

"I want them to come," Eva said. "But nobody setting foot inside that church house in no stiff shirt and epaulette, no blasted brass button and medal. Nobody. I rather see the boys with them baggy jeans hanging off they high black asses." Here was a glimpse of the brash Eva that Naomi had predicted the first night. "Lord Jesus. All yuh don't want to see what I will do to the first one who lose the key to his brain and come wearing army clothes."

Eva refused a military funeral, too. At first she thought she didn't want a funeral at all, but her years of churchgoing wouldn't let her drift that far afield. Still, she was adamant, "No flag, no uniform, none-a that army music."

There would be no burial either, no final graveside farewell. The church deacon had pointed out that "the Army benefits would pay for the nicest cemetery plot." But, Eva sucked her teeth in response. "Benefits? Burying my one boy child, that is a benefit?"

Eva considered laying Roderick out in jeans and sneakers, a team jersey with layers of T-shirts, but in the end, she agreed to a sports jacket that he liked to wear on special dates. Once, Eva had asked him to wear it to church with her, but Roderick hadn't been to church since he was fourteen. The last big argument they had was Eva trying to force him to attend service, Roderick resisting. "Ma, you know if I walk in that church one minute, they'll have me engaged to marry three different women five minutes later." Eva let Roderick win that battle, but she wished that she'd argued with him one more time after that.

The funeral went according to Eva's dictates. Roderick's

friends did come, none of them in baggy jeans, but none of them in uniform either. The casket was not draped with Old Glory. Taps was not played. The belief among family and friends was that if any words like "glory" or "honour" or "hero" were so much as spoken, Eva would explode – transform from composed grieving mother into apoplectic, inconsolable relic.

Roderick was cremated.

Eva wanted to wait for the ashes after the funeral, but despite her strongest arguments she was told that this was not possible. The professionals had seen this before – family members who wanted to see everything, wanted to stay with the remains as long as possible – so they had been kind and they arranged for "expedited delivery".

The day after the funeral, Eva awoke tired, her body sore as she stood under the strong pressure of the shower. Before she dressed, she called TransQuick, the local taxi service, and on her way out the door, she announced to Naomi that she would be "coming back just now." Naomi had taken an extra day off work to make sure that Eva wouldn't be at home alone. Partly concerned, partly annoyed Naomi wondered, *Just where Eva going? What so important this morning?* But Eva gave her sister no chance to comment.

The cab driver, Eduardo, pulled up to the curb just as Eva walked out the front door. He'd almost refused this fare when the dispatcher radioed it out. Eduardo didn't like cemeteries. He was uncomfortable with anything related to death. He'd grown up in the Dominican Republic, deep in the countryside near the border with Haiti. As a boy he'd heard more than his fair share of superstitions about death and the afterlife, from both Hispanic and *Kreyol* culture. An extra dose, indeed, once his older siblings discovered his discomfort. But business this morning was slow – the weather was bright and warm, and people who normally called TransQuick evidently felt that they could walk, or take the bus. So Eduardo took the cemetery trip.

Still, he was ready to drive away if the fare turned out to be a woman dressed *Voudoux* or *Santeria* style, all in white with sashes and beads and a banded head. But Eva looked normal, casual – blue jeans and a pink sweater. She wasn't dressed for a funeral, and she wasn't carrying flowers for a graveside visit. Eduardo concluded she wasn't on her way to do anything directly related to death, maybe just handling some financial transaction for a friend.

In the taxi, Eva's manner put Eduardo further at ease. As they pulled onto Jamaica Avenue, she asked him to turn on the radio, her West Indian accent thick. "What is that rap station all-yuh young people always blasting? Hot something-or-de-other. Put on that one." So driving through Queens, Eduardo and Eva talked about hip-hop, Eduardo naming tracks and artists, even explaining differences between regional styles.

He wasn't happy, though, when Eva directed him to drive deep into the cemetery. They stopped in front of a building that elsewhere would have looked sleek and modern, but here looked abstract and creepy. As Eva walked in, Eduardo imagined sitting in the sedan on a foggy day or a moonlit night and he was glad now that it was a bright sunny day. He hoped that Eva would keep her word, that she'd be "coming right, right back."

Mr. Harris, the director of the facility, knew that Eva would show up right at ten. He'd told her that ten was the earliest possible time that the "cremains" could be ready. They were ready, packaged in the Bolivian rosewood urn that she'd chosen. It was one of the priciest options because of the exotic wood and hand craftsmanship, yet it was one of the simplest – all in all, not a popular choice. Mr. Harris liked Eva for the choice, for her tough style of mourning, and for being right on time as he expected. He didn't know that Eva had skipped breakfast and brushed by her sister in order to be there on time, but he would not have been surprised. Mr. Harris hadn't expected Eva in jeans though, and he was almost shocked by the baseball cap. But, ever the professional, he composed his features, deciding that the cap must have belonged to the deceased.

With a couple of quick signatures, Eva was soon "right back" to Eduardo in the taxi. Luckily, he didn't know that the tote bag was now heavier, that he was carrying two passengers instead of one.

On the drive back, Eva had little to say. She spoke for the first time when they neared her home, asking what the fare would be. When she paid, she said, "Keep the change driver", giving Eduardo a generous tip, and saying, as she stepped out the car, "Don't ever let yuh children join the service, eh. Don't let them join up at all."

Eva spent the rest of the day with Naomi, who didn't bother to ask what the pressing errand had been. Again the wide berth. They watched *The Price Is Right*, offering competing bids during the games. Naomi made lunch – a thick Trinidadian soup – which the sisters ate while watching their favourite soap operas.

Eva went to work the next day. Skirt and blouse, stockings. The bus to the F-train to midtown. Service elevator down two levels to the linen room at the hotel. Her co-workers were thoughtful, solicitous, but it was back to work. Phones to answer, uniforms to repair, clean sheets and towels to shelve. Eva's trusty tote bag sat atop her desk.

A week passed. Eva went back and forth to work, to church. Eva dressed appropriately for each occasion, but always took her bag.

Inside the bag was the beautiful wood box, its edges rounded, its surface lacquered to a near-reflective gloss, smooth as river rocks. At night, alone in her bedroom, Eva would run her hands along the top, curl her fingers under the edges, rub the corners. Sometimes, too, she would do this in the seclusion that crowded rush-hour trains provided. She would imagine – close her eyes and imagine – that she had carried this cask for years, worn the wood smooth with her touch, made it shine with oil her pores had secreted. Birthed it.

A couple of weeks, a month passed. Co-workers, friends and family no longer felt they had to be extra nice. Eva was "fine, just fine." Eva believed that too.

She began taking walks during her lunch, random excursions around midtown. In Times Square one day, Eva walked right past the Army Recruitment Center and looked in. She could just as easily have been walking on the other side of 43rd Street, or on the next block over. She could have been looking up at the giant underwear billboard or glancing at the tourist couple snapping photos, but as she passed the center, she looked in and saw two men talking. Two men in uniform – the modern camouflage, soft olive and pale blue and sandy brown mottled like a designer print. Eva stood watching the men. Examining the careful fit of their garments. The heft and texture. Crisp fabric over toned bodies. Smooth at the shoulders and back, gathered at the elbows and wrists. Eva looked at the men, at the expressions changing their faces, smiles flaming and fading, arms and legs and torsos moving in gesture. Beautiful men. Strong men. Young. Alive.

Eva was late getting back to work that day.

The next day, she planned ahead: ten minutes to eat a sandwich at her desk; ten minutes to walk there and ten minutes back; fifteen minutes to spend looking in the window. It still annoyed her when management called it a lunch hour. "All a them big-time title, Executive This and Director of That and they eh know it take sixty minutes to make a hour."

Other than the timing of her luncheon trips, Eva had no plan. The visits became a routine, the routine became a comfort. She awoke in the mornings and went to work. That's what people did. As a girl in rural Trinidad, she knew the early morning whistle of the sugar factory that signalled the parade of her neighbours heading to work – men and women, old and young. She saw other luckier ones with office jobs in Town dressed neatly, but still headed to the main road to catch a taxi and squeeze inbetween other travellers. Her mother had no need to travel, but awoke to a cycle of labour: unending washing and ironing, fowls to be fed and eggs to be collected, flour to be kneaded, produce to be toted from the market.

So Eva dressed and went to work, though she needed Roderick's ashes with her to make the trip. Increasingly, too, she needed the midday visits, needed to stand in front of the plate glass and see the soldiers in their muted camouflage, going about their routines.

After a while, Sergeant Palmer and Corporal Dennis noticed Eva. In the bustle of Times Square it took them almost a week. Corp. Dennis picked her up first but said nothing.

Dennis was a strawberry-blond from the cornfields of Iowa. Plopped down in the middle of New York, at the crossroads of the world, he understood that his observations were sometimes "culturally insensitive" – the term used in a diversity training seminar he'd attended. The seminar cleared up for Dennis how some platoon-mates had reacted to state-ments he'd made early in his army life. He learned to avoid comments about certain hairstyles and grooming, he knew to avoid discussions about some political issues. So Dennis thought that it best not to mention the African American female's unusual behaviour. Anyway, she didn't fit the pro-tester profile – she was always alone, had no placard or lighted candle, and wore no buttons or ribbons.

Palmer saw Eva and he too said nothing. Palmer's parents had migrated to New York from Guyana, and Eva reminded him of his father's sister back in Georgetown. He'd feel like a traitor to point out her recurring visits to Dennis. Palmer also decided that Eva was not a troublemaker.

The day Palmer and Dennis eventually spoke with Eva, rain had been falling since the previous evening. A mist, drizzle. Spritz, as New Yorkers say. By morning there was a wet pall draped over the city. Every outdoor surface was covered with flowing beads of rain and pools formed in potholes and dents and overflowed in unison, as if on cue. In this rain, Eva appeared at her regular time in front of the Army

Recruitment Center. Eva in a rain-slick, holding a too-small umbrella, staring in. Roderick's ashes were in an extra plastic bag inside Eva's tote.

Dennis was sitting at the desk close to the front door shuffling papers (though he wouldn't have used that term if asked what he was doing); Palmer was making calls to high school seniors from a list. Eva was staring in.

"Didn't think she'd show today," Dennis said. "Not in this."

"Doesn't look like she'll melt though," Palmer said, his expression confusing Dennis.

Just as Eduardo the taxi driver knew that rainy days were good for his receipts, Palmer and Dennis knew that rainy days were good for recruiting. People came in out of the rain and that gave the soldiers time to talk. More people stayed at home too, so phone contacts had a higher percentage of success.

Roderick had first talked to a recruiter on a rainy day. After work, without an umbrella, he'd lingered in the mall, gauging the intensity of a downpour, measuring the distance between raindrops and wishing that he'd worn boots instead of new white kicks. But teenage boys don't listen to weather forecasts. He'd hung around long enough for the recruiter to ask, "Ever thought about getting Uncle Sam to pay for college?"

Roderick figured he'd kill some time. "Nobody named Uncle Anything ever paid for nothing for me before, yo. And only thing I got from my aunties was corny clothes and a bible," Roderick's grin signalled fun. He knew the value of a customer who could make a joke, or take a joke, at the end of a long day. And he'd seen the commercials. *What's ole sarge gonna say to me anyway,* he thought: *'Go Army Strong!'*?

Roderick was right, Sergeant Vincent did need a laugh. But

Roderick didn't factor in the possibility of a genuine connection. Sgt. Vincent hadn't expected it either. He'd acted the role before, pretended to bond with potential recruits, even ones he disliked.

But there was Roderick, a funny guy, popular in school, even with teachers when he was blowing off their classes. A quick hit at the Radio Shack with managers and with customers. And there was Vincent, a classic underachiever in high school – lots of girlfriends and parties and very little homework. It made sense that Roderick and Vincent hit it off. So in addition to the standard lists of opportunities, the stories about days drier and better than this one, Vincent meant it when he said that the Roderick would do well in the army.

Eva remembered the rain – rain, rain, rain – the night when Roderick came to her with the army idea. She remembered her feet feeling damp even as Roderick talked about the plans that he'd developed with the recruiter. She should not have let her son make a decision in that rain. She should have remembered that pigeon peas are planted on the feast of Corpus Christi and cassava is never planted during a new moon. And you don't plan your life on a rainy night. Standing in Times Square, looking in at Dennis and Palmer, she thought, *Why I didn't listen to the rain? My mother teach me better than that.*

But Roderick had been so excited as he asked her for permission. His facts orderly, figures at the ready. Expectant, looking forward to something for the first time in a while. In truth, Eva had been worrying about him. Roderick was not the type of boy to complain, but the bloom was off the rose at Radio Shack. A mother could tell. He couldn't go on working there his whole life. This expecting, this looking forward was something that had always struck her as very American. Engagement rings and college funds, rsvp cards. She hadn't grown up with expectations; she knew about posting banns and getting married right after, about unexpected scholarships for special students or parents simply scraping together enough money for school books; she knew about cooking a little extra because anybody might show up anytime. So sometimes Eva had worried that she hadn't been a good American mother, hadn't given her son that gift of looking forward.

In fact, when Roderick mentioned the army, Eva's thoughts had gone back to the Trinidad of her youth. A neighbour, Neville, joined the Trinidad Regiment and it had caused a tiny whirlwind in their village. Neville was only a few years older than Eva, who was still in school. The fellas his age had patted him on the back, draped proud arms across his seemingly broader shoulders; his village "aunties" and "uncles" wished him good luck and his mother walked around with her head held just a bit higher. Neville did well in the Regiment: his shoulders did grow broader, and he learned to play the trumpet. When the Regiment Band played for holidays there was Neville in his wonderful uniform, starched and pressed, his wide leather belt almost as shiny as his brass buttons.

It was Neville's uniform that Eva pictured that night. Perhaps all the years in the hotel linen room and sewing for private clients on weekends had skewed her perspective. She'd pictured Roderick starched and ironed, brass buttons gleaming, when she should have been thinking about bullets and land mines, about pigeon peas and cassava. About rain.

Eva had listened to the whole story about Sgt. Vincent, the jokes and the Army slogans, the benefits, the travel. Roderick had cajoled, "Ma, you know how smooth I am, you know I'll be okay. Sgt. Vincent said I won't be fighting, I'll be doing all tech stuff. And wait 'til I come out, we'll be set."

All she could reply was, "Boy, what I could tell yuh? I don't know nothing about no army, and less than nothing about high tech business. You know that, Roderick."

Roderick did know. He knew that her "What I could tell yuh" meant "yes". When he had kissed her cheek, they were both smiling.

Walking into the Times Square Army Recruitment Center, out of the steady rain, Eva thought of that kiss, tried to remember where exactly on her cheek it had fallen, how the lips had felt, what small whiff of her son had rushed past her nose.

"Corporal Dennis, ma'am." He was relieved to see she looked so calm and normal.

"Sergeant Palmer, Sergeant Michael Palmer."

"Evangeline Leonard."

"Would you like some coffee, Ms. Leonard?" Palmer asked. "Tea?"

"I just wanted to say hello," Eva replied. "I have to go back to work."

"Is there something we can do for you, ma'am?" Dennis asked.

"No, no, no. I just wanted to hear the sound . . . I wanted to see . . . well to meet you."

"Yes, ma'am."

After days of Eva staring in, days of Palmer and Dennis pretending not to notice, they were face to face. Touching, shaking hands. Each feeling some familiarity bred from Eva's curious routine.

Dennis thought back to his first weeks in New York, remembered meeting NJGAMR1 with whom he'd chatted and played games on-line for months before. NJGAMR1 knew things about Dennis that his family and friends didn't. Standing this close to Eva, Dennis felt that there was something she knew about him, something he knew about her. Personal things, though he couldn't begin to name them.

Palmer, for his part, had bet himself, the moment Eva had walked in the door, that he could pinpoint which Caribbean country she was from.

Eva didn't know what she had in mind. She just wanted to talk to the men. During her previous lunchtime visits, Eva had tried disliking them, hating them for signing up mother's sons – daughters too, because she'd seen girls go in and out the door on occasion. Eva wanted to be angry as she stood there. She wanted a target. But she could see Dennis and Palmer only as two men doing their jobs day after day, joking with each other, being men. It made Eva wonder what Roderick had done, had been made to do, over there in the cradle of civilization – that's what she'd learned in school, the Tigris and the Euphrates: The Cradle of Civilization, though no one called it that any more; not in the newspapers or on TV.

She prayed silently, *Lord, forgive my child his trespasses. I don't know what trespasses, but forgive him his trespasses as we forgive those...*

She turned and started toward the door.

"Miss Leonard?" Palmer said.

"Ma'am..." Dennis said, almost at the same time.

"Oh gosh, I'm sorry yes. I just wanted to come in and . . ." Eva's sentence lingered as her hand touched the door handle.

"My boy was in the army too, my son Roderick."

"Yes Ma'am." Dennis and Palmer said together.

"Nice boys," Eva said walking back into the rain.

She didn't go back the next day or the day after. It took a conscious effort to stay away, but she decided that it was important not to return.

But days without her lunchtime routine left her feeling unanchored, directionless. No one else saw the mist, felt the chill, but Eva knew that she needed to break through the fog that surrounded her. She called Stella and asked if Chad could come over at the weekend. She asked Chad too. "I need a computer refresher, this rusty old-lady brain don't remember half what you show me." Eva's plan was to take Chad shopping. Treat him for helping with the emails. Treat herself, by just being around him.

Naomi had done all of the cooking since the night when she served *pelau* to Corporal Parks and the senior officer. But Eva planned to cook a special lunch for Chad. Before Roderick left for the army, Eva had cooked once or twice each week – curried chicken, stewed oxtails, macaroni pie – Roderick's favourites. Saturday's lunch would be stewed oxtails.

After work on Friday, Eva went to both the greengrocer's and the supermarket. She'd bumped into the same young man in both places and she'd heard him asking advice about an ingredient for a meal he was cooking for his beau – though she hadn't guessed that he was cooking for a man. She'd been conscious that she'd caught the young man's attention. Perhaps he'd sized her up as a good cook. In truth, the young man was more than a little curious about Eva's plans. *Looks like the old girl's holding it down for the seniors. Wish I could get Maman to go on a date.* He didn't know how far off he was. Eva hadn't had a date since Roderick was in grade school.

She'd had had her share of beaus, starting with Neville from the Trinidad Regiment, but she hadn't seen much point in men after Roderick's father disappeared. The handful of times she went out after, with this "gentleman" or that "fella" – never the same one twice – had been concessions. Eventually, she told her friends and family that she was done with "all-a that stupidness." Stella's husband had commented: "Yes, I know, she too old! Diana Ross and Joan Collins could get married, ten, twenty years older than she, but Evangeline too old."

Stella and her husband dropped off Chad late Saturday morning. Eva had remembered that teenage boys hate to get up early on weekends, so the lesson was scheduled for noon. Chad helped her with email again, and they sent out thank-you's to the people they'd sent out announcements to during her second lesson. While they worked, Eva fished for information about what clothes Chad liked. When Roderick was in high school, he always seemed to want a new pair of jeans, a new version of some sneaker or boot or something. Eva figured she'd get Chad something like that.

But Chad didn't care about clothes and fashion. "I'm saving up my allowance for games," he told Eva. "Granddad's got me on a no-games restriction, so it's a forced savings, actually." Eva bit her tongue, she had long imagined that living with her brother-in-law was a form of torture, but far be it from her to interfere.

Still, the afternoon went well. Chad didn't know that the lesson was a ruse and Eva never realized that Chad didn't like oxtails. After lunch, they headed out to the mall. It was a bright day in late spring and everyone on the Q29 bus had something to look forward to. Gianni and Gina were going to a movie that he'd let her choose (and he was looking forward to them being too otherwise occupied to see); Landon and his friends were going to sneak into the R-rated movie that Gianni really wanted to see; Deshawn was getting his ear pierced; and, Mrs. Quinones was going to buy a layette for the birth of her first granddaughter.

In the mall, Eva and Chad passed by people who weren't quite as glad to be there – Marie, being fitted for a striped satin bridesmaid dress that looked like a sofa slipcover; Leroy, the greying security guard, being bawled out by the young store manager; and Sgt. Vincent, the army recruiter, who was lagging far behind his monthly target – but Eva and Chad were on a mission of their own.

The comic book store was different from what Eva imagined. No Crayola colours, no Betty and Veronica. The store was well lit, yet felt dark: customers in deep blue jeans and dark T-shirts, rows and rows of grim-covered novels and magazines. Still, Chad looked even happier there than he did in front of the computer screen. He talked to the other customers and the store clerk, and though Eva could make neither hide-nor-hair of what they were saying, watching them buzz around made her happy.

Afterwards, Chad wanted to go to the video-game store. "I just want to see what's out there, or by the time my restriction's over I'll be completely obsolete," he said.

"Oh my gosh! Obsolete, like your poor old aunt," Eva felt good enough to joke.

"You're not obsolete Auntie, you're vintage."

The fog was lifting.

Chad met a friend from school on the escalator and Eva let them go off on their own for a while. She still had visions of buying Chad some clothes. The comic books had cost a lot of money, but Eva couldn't but think of them as disposable.

Outside the video-game store, across the way from Radio Shack where Roderick had worked, Sgt. Vincent had set up his table. He hoped that moving from his usual spot near the mall entrance might change his luck, and if not his luck then at least the scenery.

Fifteen minutes later, Eva headed to meet Chad, as planned. She was carrying a bag with two graphic tees and a baseball cap. She was happy with her purchase. She took little note of the group of boys milling around outside the store.

"Auntie Eva!"

She looked closer and saw a half-dozen young men around a table. It was covered with glossy papers that looked like credit card applications, or travel brochures. She saw Chad and Ramesh, the boy with whom she'd left him. Ramesh looked older than Chad by a year or two. She saw Sgt. Vincent, smiling. Sgt. Vincent was a handsome man when he smiled – young-looking. The group that Eva saw all looked like teenagers.

Chad called her again, waved. She wasn't sure if he was waving her over or bidding her wait, but as she walked over she saw that Chad was smiling too. She saw Sgt. Vincent's arm reach up and fall and, as casual as a playground game, his right hand landed on Chad's shoulder. His left hand was already on Ramesh's shoulder. Eva saw the uniform as if for the first time, the epaulettes.

"Chad! Boy, what the devil..."

"Auntie Eva, we're just hanging out with the sergeant..."

"This dude's got jokes," Ramesh said.

"Chad, that is not what I brought you to..."

"Ma'am," Sgt. Vincent piped up in his most official, most placating tone. "Just chatting with these fine young men."

Eva snatched Chad by the elbow, leaving the officer's hand temporarily afloat. She could feel eyes on her and she didn't care. She grabbed Ramesh too – he was no relative of hers but she had no intention of leaving him there.

"Ma'am, there's no need to..." Sgt. Vincent began.

"Need? Yes there is a need. You have a need."

"Ma'am..."

"And you think that my nephew have a need..."

"Auntie Eva we could just go... Let's go."

"Well, I have a need. You want to know what my need is?" Eva read the recruiter's name – she was getting good at that. "Sergeant Vincent, here is my need." Eva put her tote on the table, slid her hand inside, and found the urn in the space that she knew so well.

"Here is my need."

Eva pulled the lacquered box out, put it on the table. She stopped and looked around at each member of the group. Took her time. The crowd had grown. Eva saw a boy in a Radio Shack uniform. Her fingers caressed the wood as they had for weeks.

"I need you to meet... I need ... all of you ... to meet my son."

Ramesh's smile had faded completely. Chad looked scared.

"This is my only son, Roderick. Private First Class, Roderick Leonard. Meet my son."

INTO MY PARLOUR

I walk down the road, up the steps and into my house, shaking my head, just shaking my head all the way. Really and truly that woman make me so angry. I'm going back and forth between thinking about her damn bold-facedness and trying to keep my blood pressure down. I head straight back to the kitchen and set down the container of half-shelled pigeon peas on the counter.

One thing I'll tell yuh: she wouldn't a try this kinda thing when my husband was still alive. That is how people like she does take advantage of people like me. In the thirty something years that I living here on Reed Street with Emelda Johnson, she and I was never no set of friends, nothing more than "Morning Miss 'Melda" and "Howdy do Miss Betty". I know I don' have nobody to blame but myself, but I still can't believe that I end up inside her house today, where she feel she could mind my business and wash her mouth on my family.

But now that I sit down by this kitchen window with some breeze on my face, I realize that is trick she trick me. She well take time and plan out this thing, moving slow and steady like a tortoise. She start off inviting me to "come an' visit meh church one o' these Sundays" and then she want to know "Why yuh cooking, cooking all the time, when yuh could come and eat two or three days by me." Well I didn't fall for

that. My whole life I going to the Anglican Church and is now she expect me to go to some wayside save-your-soul church? Eh-eh. And I don't have to eat her food either, I could still afford to buy my own and I have health and strength to prepare it too, praise God.

Well I better wash my hands and get something to drink before my blood get hot again, yes ... Let me fill up this glass with ice all the way to the top ... and let me splash in some Angostura bitters ... Yes is like I cooling off already just watching the bitters streaking down over the ice cubes. That woman will not get the best of me. In fact, you know what? I could just pour out the ice from this everyday glass into one of my special glasses from The States. Yes now, that really looking nice, crystal inside more crystal. Add some sparkling tonic water, and I good.

You see, is just jealousy that have Emelda so. Her son Ainsley leave Reed Street and gone to Canada long before my nephew (dear boy) gone to The States, and all she have to show for it is that picture of his wife and children playing in the snow. And she always pushing it in somebody face, talking about her daughter-in-law this, and her grandchildren that. Well.

Yet I still end up agreeing to go and make market with her. After all, today is not like yesterday, and a woman my age can't all the time be moving about the place alone. Is good to have some company to go downtown San Fernando in the early morning. To tell the truth that arrangement work out okay, except for the fact that she so damn cheap that she always have to try to get the people to add in an extra lime to the heap, or reduce the price of their yam. But that didn't have anything to do with me; I just pay the people price and say thank God.

Now today make two-three trips like that, and I end up agreeing to cross that woman doorstep when we reach back here on Reed Street. "Miss Betty, since the taxi drop we off right by my door, why yuh don' come inside and shell the peas by me one time?" she say. And is only studying that "Yes, the peas does shell so much easier when they fresh" that make me say, "All right." And *whattap*! I fall right in she trap. How the saying does go? Come into my parlour said the spider to the fly. I was the fly on Reed Street this morning.

No sooner than I shell the first pod of peas, she start off talking like if I am some lonely old woman: "Yuh don' fin' de peas dem does shell much faster when yuh have lil company while you doin' it?" But in truth, she make me remember how since Terrance was a little boy, he used to like to sit down with me, and help me shell. The two of us could get through five pounds like nothing – as long as he didn't see a worm.

"Boy, once the first, fat peas-worm show up, Terrance done shelling." I was thinking about that and laughing and then I realize that I was saying it out loud to Emelda.

Well who tell me to say that?

"Girl you was lucky, yes," she jump in right away, "I never could get Ainsley to help me with nothing so, he was always running a football or playing pitch somewhere in the road." When she see I didn't respond to that she continue, "And now I sure your nephew could well cook and thing, an Ainsley have to wait for his wife to do all o' that for him." I didn't pay her any mind, just kept shelling the peas. But it was too late, I already give her the opening she want.

"Yuh nephew was never one to be out playing with the fellas. I even uses to see him helping you sew and thing so too."

I start to tell her that this is modern times now, ask her what is wrong with a male child being able to fend for himself, but I wouldn't waste my breath on that woman.

Look, you see? She have me getting riled up again. I won't have that at all. I know just the thing… Put on some good, Christian music… as a matter of fact, this nice gospel tape from The States… Yes Lord, 'Rock-a my soul in the bosom of Abraham'. Yuh think that old spider woman have anybody to remember what she like and send her Hezekiah Walker music and a card with pretty pink flowers for her birthday?

I could ask her questions so, when she starts talking, but I'm not that kind of woman. I don't have it in my heart. You have to be hardhearted to behave like Emelda, yes. Imagine that she feel she could talk to me so: "Girl, yuh nephew eh married yet… But how old he is now? He must be over thirty already … Anyway, I sure he not getting into all that kinda slackness I hear does be goin' on in New York… But at the same time, he better start havin' some lil grandniece and grandnephew for yuh while yuh could enjoy them."

Lord, once she get started is like she eat parrot-ass-and-garlic, she just keep talking, talking: "Is already too late for yuh husband to see dem… That man work so hard, day and night, and he come an' drop down and leave yuh so… I couldn't take the strain that I see yuh going through."

"You lucky in truth, yes 'Melda." I couldn't help myself. "Well lucky never to have to worry with husband problems for all theses years."

The woman was carrying on like if I ever ask her to put food on my table, like if I ever once knock on her door bawling and crying. But as I say, I not going to let that woman send my pressure up. I changing out of these tight clothes and getting comfortable and cool… Yes this nice shorts-and-top that I get for Mother's Day. Terrance always thinking about his old aunt, yes. If I had carry him in my own belly for nine months he couldn't be more like a son to me. Look how nice this little outfit looking on me. He always used to say that he like to see me wearing nice bright colours, little lemon-yellow and peach and thing. Even though he gone all these years, when he send me something I could see he didn't forget his Aunt Betty.

Now that I'm relaxed, let me go and carry back that woman container. I walk out of her house so fast before that I forget that I had the pigeon peas in her bowl. But I'm not going to give her the chance to tell all of Reed Street that I keeping her things… Let me rinse it out and dry it good… she wouldn't be able to say I bring back her bowl dirty, either. And even though I know she will find something to say about my rose-coloured T-shirt, that is her business. I don't have time for all of that.

"Miss Emelda…" (Watch, she will take her time to come and answer me, like if she can't hear me) … "Miss Emelda, is me… Well my dear, thanks again for going to the market with me… No love, I not going to come in, I just wanted to bring your bowl back in case you need to use it… Oh gosh, now that I'm standing here I realize how loud I have my music next door; I hope it not bothering you… This thing, girl? You know how long Terrance send me this from New York… But thanks… Okay then, I running back home. I promise myself to make some phone calls and catch up with my business."

I reach back inside and I'm feeling much better, because I

know I didn't let that woman get the best of me. Let me make a little phone call while it fresh on my mind. I know I will get the voice machine, but I just want to call and hear Terrance voice: *Please leave a message after the beep and I will call you back.*

"Terrance darling, this is your Auntie Betty, but you realize that already. Boy, I just calling to say hello. You know you don't have to call me back like you say on the message. Instead of making overseas calls I rather you save up your money and spend it on a plane ticket. Well, you aunt doing quite fine, just putting up with these people down here, you know how it is. I relaxing listening to that nice gospel tape you send me, and I just decide to make a quick call. I hope you doing well up there in the cold. I know you must be have some nice young lady to help keep you warm by now. Maybe the next time you come down will be on your engagement trip or on a honeymoon. Anyway, take care, okay. God bless."

ON THE SIDE

Leigh is lying on me. His legs are still on the passenger side, I guess, but I can't see them because that whole side is pushed in, mashed and crumpled into this tiny little space that seems too small. But his legs are there. I feel cold.

I tell him, "Leigh, the cops are gonna come and put flares down in the road."

I feel cold and sleepy. His waist is kinda on the gearshift box, his chest is on my side, and his head is on my chest, warm against my chest. He's wearing my bandana with the Trinidad colours, and he's so close to me – close to my mouth, close to my nose – that I smell the espresso he had earlier.

I tell him, "You know those little pink flares they put on the road, real pretty right, little salmon stars. The other night when I was going home I saw some a block away from me on Myrtle, they looked like party lights on the road, like lights by a pool for a grand little pool party." But it wasn't a party, only an accident.

The cops will come. And the ambulance. Then what? Then Lester – shit – Lester with questions: What was I doing with his man in the middle of the night? With his man and driving his car? "We just went to the diner." Why was I driving? Lester won't get it. That's what we do, Leigh and I. We eat in diners. It just happened like that. "Right babe?"

★

When we started again, after I saw him in the bar, we went to Junior's.

"That's where you live? You right near Junior's, yo," Leigh says. "I know you be getting your cheesecake on. . . on the regular."

I tell him I haven't been to Junior's in years.

"That's it. I'm coming by there tonight. We going."

When we get there, Leigh grabs the red plastic handle on the big glass door and waits while I walk in out of the drip-drip drizzle that's been greying up the whole day.

"After you, baby," he says, and gives me his grin.

We walk in and it's bright inside: red, and red and white. The famous cheesecakes are there in a special counter by the door – plain and pineapple and strawberry and blueberry, they're lined up in the cases, from the little six-inch ones to the big party-size, ready to be boxed up in those candy-cane striped, bakery boxes. We pass cherry-topped vinyl stools at the counter on the way to the hostess stand. A middle-aged woman with a red and white apron greets us and walks us to a booth in the back, a red booth in the back.

"You're gonna like this waitress," he tells me. "She's real cool, ya know, like a big sister or a moms, ya know."

When she comes back and takes his order, and they do their little regular-customer/special-waitress thing, I can see him being the little boy in the big Tims, and I see her being charmed. She wears her hair in a short natural like my mother's friend Hyacinth, who kissed me once in a dream in the back of a cab.

"So, you like them Trini women, eh?" I say to Leigh while we wait for the food.

He says, "I told you, she's good people."

After we start eating – he's got pancakes and scrambled eggs with cheese and a side of sausages, I'm too hopped up to eat my cheeseburger, so I nibble at the fries – after we start eating, he tells me she reminds him of Lester's mother.

"But Lester's Guyanese," I say.

"No, he's Trini too." Leigh looks at me – I mean he's been looking at me all night – but now he gives me the direct, full power look. "Can I share something with you?"

He waits, not going forward – though the question is really only a preface – but waiting for an answer.

"Can I?"

"Please," I nod.

"Every man I've ever had in my life was from Trinidad."

"Really," I say. "Guess once you go Trini, you never want a Yankee."

He screws his face up at my bad joke, but laughs anyway. And shares. Shares why he and Lester broke up six months ago. Shares how close they had become: special because it was nothing special, ya know; built a home together in Jersey, bought stuff, cared for each other, met each other's family – men and women do it every day, right? I remember all those years ago when I had done all of that too, been part of the model gay couple, the couple our friends told their friends about. I remember how hard it was when I lost it too.

"I'm glad I touched you in the bar last night," I say, because I don't just want to say 'I know, I know'.

But I give up on eating any more. Three-quarters of the

burger sits next to the ketchup on the white plate. And when Leigh says, "Take a ride uptown with me," do I know that I'll let him take me to Harlem with him even though we're five blocks from my studio? Take me to Harlem to the studio that he got when he had to leave the home he built with his man. Take me uptown, and let him, let him take me?

★

I wake up. There's an ambulance behind us. It's a big, old, ugly truck, square and hard, like an evil Transformer toy, grown up. I'm still cold. The ambulance's flashing lights are on, like big monster eyes spitting fire, blinking from dark to blinding red, back and forth, dark to red, dark to red. Now an EMT is standing at the car, at Lester's car, looking in the window at me and Leigh. I hear his radio, crackling and squawking, and when he shines a flashlight in, I see us now, the shattered window, the hole where the windshield should be.

"Sir, can you hear me," he says. "Sir."

"Yeah," I say, but it's rough and garbled like "Yrrh".

When he plays the light in the car and waves it around and over us, I see the glass everywhere – the dashboard is covered with it, and the hood and inside too, it's on me, on my legs, on Leigh, all over him. Not flat and sharp like splinters, but rough and crumbly looking. Decorating everything like sprinkles on a Mr. Frosty cone, because each piece is picking up some light and flicking it back at my eyes with a different colour: Detroit metal green from the hood, denim blue from my jeans, white and yellow from the lights, dark red from the bandana, bright red. Shit! Bright red from my arm, from Leigh's face and arm and leg. Bright, blood red from Leigh's body.

"Help us, look at him," I say to the EMT.

"Okay sir, okay. We're going to take care of you."

★

The first time Leigh shows up in Lester's car I should have guessed it wasn't his own, because he makes a point of asking me to grab cd's, even though I know he practically has a cd library in his car. But I'm still grooving on how he looks, on how good he looks. When he had called earlier he was at his sister getting his hair braided.

"You might like it. . . I don't know," he teased. "It's different from the way I always have it."

He 'always' has it back in cornrows, maybe a dozen cornrows, neat from forehead to neck, sleek from temple to nape. They were like that when I first him five years ago – before Lester. When I met him at Sound Factory Bar, because that was the place back then. I remember the attitude – tough and hard and scary. Hard when he stepped over to me, baggy denim overalls over nothing but Tims, tough all the way when he walked with me to the coat-check downstairs, scary, trying to be scary when he moved me into the corner and got his face in mine.

"Yo, don't forget to call me, okay? Okay? Leigh." Then he said it again, "Leigh", and touched his lips to my lips in the dark corner. I remember.

When he shows up tonight, I gotta groove on the look.

"You got me cheesin, son," I pull him in the door.

"You like it, like my hair?"

I grin.

"Do it fit my face and everything?"

"Yeah," I say, liking the small cornrows twisted tight around in many jagged parts. Liking the hair and loving the brown coveralls that he's wearing. "Nice," I think.

"Yeah, you look real nice," I say. And I kiss him at the door.

★

The cops are here now. They came just as the EMTs were getting me out of the car. I see cars slow down to rubberneck as they go by. I'm doing my calm, crisis-management thing, but I know that it won't last much longer, because it's really a fake and I can't remember what the EMTs look like. I need them to get Leigh out of the car and take care of him. The cops sit me down on a kind of built-in bench in the back of the ambulance and I can tell that they're managing me, keeping the situation under control. They ask questions, but they're not the ones I expect. They don't ask "Where are you coming from?" or "What is your relationship?" or "Who's his next of kin?" They're filling in the paperwork – date and time and last-name-first; they're keeping me away from the flat, paddle-like board and the oversized neck-brace that the EMTs are using on Leigh.

★

"What are you saying?" Leigh asks. "Huh, that you don't want to do this?"

The Downtown Brooklyn Diner should have been the last time. I remember the place from years ago and though they've renovated, it's still ugly. We're here because there's too much traffic to go anywhere else, hungry as we are. I don't answer him right away. Can't. It's Monday afternoon and I should not be sitting in this booth with a street sign that says Shore Parkway. There's a different sign at each booth. Cadman Plaza, where two uniformed cops sit all the way in the back, Coney Island Avenue right behind us where the Latino family sits with two small boys and a baby, forcing us to keep our voices down. I think I really need to be finding a job and handling some business – too much time on my hands.

"Or, that you want to do this one more time then never see me again."

I'm putting together everything he's said so far, thinking how I've fucked up 'cause I'm finding out now about shit I should have asked about before. Before I went uptown. Shit. Yes he and Lester broke up last October. Yes, it was ugly and vicious. Yes, he has his own place in Harlem. But they see each other again now.

"What does that mean, exactly?" I ask.

Lester spent two nights in Harlem last week... Oh yeah, and Leigh spent three nights in Jersey. Yeah, and Saturday night when I saw Leigh in the bar he had just left Jersey. I'm thinking, "You can stop now, I've heard enough."

But yeah, they were just picking at each other so he said he was going to move his car and take a little drive. And yeah, when we were sitting in the car outside the club and Leigh's cell was ringing, um yeah, it was Lester.

Yeah, "He wants us to get back together."

"He wants?"

Okay yeah, "We're talking 'bout getting back."

So what am I saying? No, I don't want to do this again. No, I want to do this one more time. No. I'm saying that all I can do right now is finish my chicken gyro, finish the grilled chicken and fried pitta that are pretty good, because you can't go wrong with grilled chicken. And if there weren't all the "yeses" and "yeahs" and "nos" tossing around in my head, I'd want a wedge of lemon to take the chicken just there. Just there, like I was for a minute, for a hot minute on Saturday when I thought I could take a shortcut, just there like on Sunday when I thought that Leigh would make a great guide.

"All, I'm saying is…"

I look over and his plate is empty. What did he order? Can I tell what he had just by looking at the empty plate? Is that gravy from the meatloaf, or barbecue sauce from chicken wings? Was that sticky looking place where mashed potatoes sat, or were they scrambled eggs?

"… Finish your coffee so we can get out of here."

★

But Brooklyn Diner wasn't the last. After another, then another it became a joke, "Where we gonna go today, son?" you asked the third time and the fourth, when you knew we'd end up at a diner again. And after it was a joke, it became a tradition that felt good, like knowing that there're gonna be presents under the Christmas tree. Then it became a contest, a challenge: "Man, we're going to a real joint today, not like that weak-assed spot you picked last week." Or, "Leigh, wait till you see the French toast they make here, it's as thick as your arm and the colour of a Trinidad sunset." Then it was just what we do. Grits and scrambled eggs at five in the morning after sweating in a club, or chicken wings and fries when we woke up at two in the afternoon after he stayed in Brooklyn, or burgers on wheat toast with mayo and tomato and no lettuce before a movie. And coffee for you, always coffee for you. Tonight you had espresso at The Seaview Cove Diner.

★

"What are you doing tonight?" Leigh asks as soon as he walks into my apartment.

And I grab him like I always do when he walks in here, always – if he hasn't called in a week and I'm on that edge between jonesing and fury; always – if he left twelve seconds ago and came back for his gum. I grab him and lean against the wall with him on me so I can put my lips right on the smooth, tight muscle over his collarbone, under his ear.

"You know what I'm doing. I'm seeing you," I say into his face.

"For real though, do you have anything to do? Do you have anywhere to be?"

And when I say no, he grins the grin I work to get, and before his kiss is over, he's dragging me out the door.

"We going for a ride, yo…"

It's not really warm enough today, but as we're on the FDR riding up past the Water Club, then the Roosevelt Island Tram, we open up the sun roof and turn up the music and Darling Nikki makes me laugh. Leigh keeps driving, through the Bronx and unto I95.

"You not hungry babe, huh?"

I shrug and he screws up his face in a double wink and says, "Good, cause by the time we get there, you'll have a big ole appetite."

I95 takes us past Stamford and Bridgeport and some other ports and then Route 2a to another road and some smaller road with a sign that tells me we're now in Rhode Island – the Ocean state. Have I ever been in Rhode Island before? When we swing into the gravel parking lot with the chunky white stones crunching under the tires, the sign that says "Seaview Cove Diner" is painted on wood in white, block letters below a faded red picture of a lobster. When we walk in, Leigh's jeans hanging off him, his cornrows peeking out the back of my Trinidad bandana that he claimed as a do-rag the first night he stayed in Brooklyn, with me trying to keep up the pace in bootleg Iceberg from Fulton Street, the joint notices, the customers quiet and the waitresses turn.

"Let's do some eating, babe," Leigh says smiling.

We start with shrimp cocktails, extra lemon and Tabasco on the side. "And leave the menus right here for us – we're gonna keep looking," Leigh tells the waitress. He tells me about his new job and thanks me for helping with his resumé. Then we order Greek salads with stuffed grape leaves and lots of feta and end up feeding the last few olives to each other. I don't pay attention to the other customers. I don't ask him why he didn't call this week. When I want to have the boffo-bacon-burger, Leigh talks me into the surf 'n' turf.

"We'll be having the same thing, babe," I try to protest. "We never get the same thing."

"Except for the coffee though," he says.

Leigh charms the waitress – when you first meet Leigh, he

either scares you or charms you – he gets her to sit with us after the diner empties out. Her name is Lola, a young grandma with a feathered pixie haircut, she comes to New York at least once a year to go shopping. They trade pictures of his kids and her grandkids. She tells me that I can't leave without having some of the apple pie *à la mode* 'cause they order them from her good girlfriend who uses fresh nutmeg "…and beside, you could use a little more meat on your bones…" and turns to Leigh with arched eyebrows "…Right?" So it's 2 a.m. and they're closing when we leave and after the espresso for Leigh and the cappuccino for me – on the house, 'cause "you've got a long drive and it's late" – we pull out of the parking lot, from the gravel onto the smooth pavement of Route 1 and Leigh is all trash talk, phone-sex talk, and I'm all soap opera tease as I push my seat back and lick my lips. By the time we're on Route 78 I have my left hand on Leigh's thigh and his right hand's inside my belt. The moon roof is open and the light is soft on Leigh's face.

★

The ambulance is square and hard inside. I watch the EMTs put Leigh on the stretcher, and I hear them on the radio with the hospital. I wonder if the blanket they've put around my shoulders is clean, and think how nice it would be to be here alone with Leigh, just us looking across at the hills in Jersey with the lights reflecting on the Hudson. I think that we wouldn't be here if I'd let him walk past in the bar that night, or if I didn't have such a heavy meal, maybe skipped the apple pie. The cops finish the accident report.

"No it's not my car." I show them my license and they find the registration behind the sun visor. "Yes, my friend Lester knows I'm driving it." It doesn't show up as stolen and they finish the report.

★

I start to drive somewhere in Rye because Leigh's started fighting with the big rigs on the road. After snaking through ten miles of construction with concrete barricades inches from the car, Leigh's agitated. He's cussing and honking with each big rig we try to get by. I don't hesitate when he asks me if I want to drive. I don't remember that it's Lester's Maxima. I don't even say that I'm glad that he trusts me to drive him, he never lets anyone drive him. I think he's calmer by the time we get back to the city. I'm driving down the Henry Hudson Parkway and Leigh's on my right, then the water, then New Jersey's hills. But when I pass the exit for 158th Street, he's pissed.

"I'm not going to your apartment, you know I'm not comfortable there."

And he's agitated again. "Why we always got to go through this?"

By the time we get to the 125th Street exit I'm not looking at him, and I reach to turn the music back on, 'cause I'm not going to listen to him either. Then there's his hand on the steering wheel turning it towards the off ramp and "What the fuck!" I react without thinking, without thinking, holding onto the wheel, yanking it to the left. Then... what? Then what? Then nothing 'til the Transformer ambulance, nothing 'til the colours.

★

They wheel Leigh to the back of the ambulance, and the stretcher's legs collapse into nothing, just like on TV. One EMT climbs in after us and the other slams the doors, one after the other. I'm looking out the little square windows in the back of the truck, over Leigh with the oxygen tubes and EMT working on him and I see Lester's car again. It's crumpled up against the ramp, with glass sprinkled around and the flares are flickering. I hear the siren start to scream and close my eyes on that image as we pull off.

TIME AND TIDE

Ten days after the car accident I leave New York and go to Trinidad – make a flight reservation and just leave. And from the time the plane comes in for a night landing, it's good. I see the lights sparkling on the coast of Port of Spain, splayed out into the Northern Mountain Range. These aren't the flashy, big-city-bright-lights of a NYC landing at Kennedy or La Guardia. They're quiet and earthy – beaconing flecks of quartz splashed deep in dark, rich stone. Good. The plane lands at Piarco and I walk out of the stale, pressurized air down the old-fashioned stairs and onto the tarmac. The tropical night air blows around my body and grabs me tight, penetrating fast though clothes and flesh, deep to the bone, wafting into my nose and deep into my lungs. Good. I think I smell sugar cane burning – and whether it's real or not – it's good.

At first I'd planned to go back "home". Spend time with my aunts and cousins being pampered and fussed over, having them cook my favourite meals. I'd pictured Auntie Betty shelling pounds and pounds of fresh pigeon peas, enough to stew some for lunch one day, with still more left to curry the next. I'd seen Aunt Phyllis and me in the backyard my first morning in Couva – even before breakfast – watering plants and picking guavas. I'd eat the green guavas with salt and

pepper, and Aunt Phyllis would make juice and jelly with the
ripe ones.

But I don't go to Couva, I check into Chaconia Inn like a
tourist. I don't let my aunts know I am in Trinidad. I can't let
them know that their "only nephew" is staying anywhere but
with one of them, or with all of them in turn – a week here and
a couple nights there.

The first day there're no guavas, but there's also no damned
phone to answer (or ignore) as messages get left on the
machine. "Hey, you okay? Holla back . . . we wanna make sure
everything's all right." How could I be? "Yeah, I'm okay." Or
maybe even, "Not so good, but I'm hanging in there". But
definitely not, "No, I'm not all right".

'Everything' is not just the accident. I know that my friends
are worried about my behaviour after the accident, but I'm
worried about my behaviour before. The physical jolt of the
crash forced me out of orbit. For how long would I have
continued seeing Leigh "on the side" if we hadn't run off the
road in his boyfriend's car? What did it mean that I was so
easily caught up with someone who wasn't mine for the
taking? The questions mount one on top of the other.

But the first day in Trinidad, the only question is, "Yuh
want the maid to straighten yuh room this morning, or later?"
Good and easy.

And the second day, another easy question, "Ey boy! Ey,
what you doing down here?"

Phillip is flowing out of a store on Frederick Street, with
one hand on the hip of his linen drawstring trousers, the other
pulling down his shades for effect. Good. That question

doesn't need an answer. It isn't the inquiry, "Why are you here?" It's the statement, "It's nice to see you".

And the next statement is, "You ain' going back before we have a chance to *lime*?" Yes, that's another easy one.

I answer with, "Nah man, I just reach."

So on my third day 'home', I'm *liming* with Phillip – practising that special Trini art of passing time without a set activity. "Listen man, don't stay at nobody's hotel," he'd said. "Yuh coming with me... I'm going up to Maracas to escape my many admirers and temptations. . . and try to finally finish some sewing I have to do." I'm comfortable around Phillip, and Maracas Bay, nestled amidst the hills of the north coast, is far from Couva, so there is no chance of my aunts finding me out. And *liming* is easier than trying to figure out why I've spent weeks convincing myself that I wasn't doing anything wrong, that I wasn't having an affair with someone else's man.

And just as I expect, Phillip fills the morning with talk of politics and his latest fashion project and good juicy gossip about no one in particular. There's no need to talk about me.

We walk on the beach and a man playing football catches my eye. He looks just like the other fellas running the ball – dressed in a beat-up pair of shorts, barefoot and barebacked with a rag sticking out his back pocket. Except, he's working some fancy footwork on the ball, moving with the ease of a coconut palm's branch in a breeze. The grin on his face matches the sweep of his legs as he puts those wicked beats on the ball. Light, reflecting off the sweat on his back, mirrors the sun flashing off the water in the bay. As he runs, his calf muscles seem to ripple in the rhythm of the cresting waves. Yeah, he is beautiful.

"See that one, that specimen there?" Phillip asks. "That's Glen Moore."

I wonder if he's telling me this because he's caught me staring, or just as a point of interest. Phillip is *liming partner* and modern day griot – drinking at Smokey's and talking some slackness about a nice-nice man one minute, and explaining the next minute that the root of the old calypso refrain '*sanie manite*' is the French phrase '*sans humanite*'.

Whatever the reason, he begins, "That's a real Trini kinda *commess* story, yuh know. His family are the Moores who own Moore Building Equipment and Contracting down south. But for the past few years he living in the woods somewhere 'round here with some woman in a shack."

Before I can tell Phillip that I went to school with a boy named Glen Moore, the fellas finish up the game. This Glen Moore walks right past me and, as my grandmother used to say, our 'eyes make four'. He walks another few feet, turns around and stares again. And I know that he's the same Glen Moore from my class at Presentation College – more than twenty years ago.

Phillip continues with the story, but it's lost between the crashing waves, and the counterpoint of blood drumming in my ears. The look on Glen's face asks, "Don't I know you?"

I answer with a pointed finger, and a smile that says, "Yeah I know you."

I feel Phillip's eyes boring into me, almost saying "Ay, ay."

Glen says, " Pres, right? Lemme see. . . You used to sit behind me. . . in form two."

★

Later Phillip and I sit on the gallery, it gets dark fast and hard, as night races past dusk. We've had a dinner of fried shark from one of the stalls down the bay and now Phillip's applying beads to a gown, his current project. A desk lamp attached to an extension cord bathes him in a spotlight as though he's on stage. I smell lime on my hands from the juice I made earlier, and the mosquito coil adds a smoky musk to the ocean breeze.

"Boy, I ain' used to seeing you without a stiff drink," I tease him.

"Dear, you just haven't seen the industrious side of me before," he flips back. "Drinking and driving – maybe. But drinking and sewing – never."

We trade lines back and forth, as I avoid talking about me, and my life. Phillip lets me get away with it. It's hard to say how long we sit there accompanied by the ocean sounds in the background. When Glen comes walking up the path, Phillip's arched eyebrows and tilted head reflect my surprise.

"Company," he says, making the word sing. "Com-pah-nee."

"Behave yourself," I tell him.

By the time Phillip gives me a response of mock innocence and an 'I-don't-know-what-you're-talking-about' look, Glen is just feet from us, close enough for us to notice the crisp whiteness of his short-sleeved shirt. Glen throws his arms out from his sides in a simple announcement of his presence.

As I fumble for something cool to say, Glen says, "Oh Gawd, all yuh don't have to watch me like I just land from outer space. Yuh didn't believe I was going to pass by?"

Phillip says, "Nah we believe yuh, and you don't look like you land from outer space, yuh just look like yuh walking into assembly at Presentation College in you nice white shirt."

I suck my teeth in a long *stewps,* and laugh, "Don't bother with him, man, come and sit down."

Glen laughs with us. "I'll tell you one thing, I never walked into Pres' with a bottle of *babash."* He pulls a flask from his back pocket.

"Yeah, Brother Michael would never stand for that," I say.

Glen sits on the brick bannister. "And Brother Michael didn't miss anything," he says.

"Not anything," I agree.

If I were in my Brooklyn apartment, I'd have put on a soul cd and lit a scented candle. But the natural sounds and light and smells – waves and stars, citrus and smoke – are all we need as we sit and talk. Sit and 'old talk'.

But soon Phillip says, "Fellas, is work I working here, so all yuh better take that *babash* and go and *lime* down on the beach."

Glen and I walk toward the surf and I hear different sections of the ocean orchestra: the booming bass of the big waves yards away from shore, the swooshing *shack-shack* beat as the water laps against the sand, sending it gently shifting; the flittering high notes as foamy bubbles burst and rejoin the salty night air.

Glen is just ahead of me, leading the way, on his own turf. I watch his back, a man's back now, but I remember the boy's back on the bench in front of me in form two – the back that held my attention while Mr. Mungal read to us on a lazy Friday afternoon, or while Brother Timothy explained the physical principles of polarity, attraction and repulsion.

We sit on a piece of driftwood and talk about those days when we did wear white shirts and go to assembly. Days when we made up nicknames for our teachers: Brother Timothy, always in a hurry, was BT express after the Hughes Corporation song; Mr. Williams our fanatic Spanish master was *Todos*, because he knew it all. I ask about Rambachan, the teacher's pet. I ask if Cole, the smartest guy in the class, became the doctor we all expected he would. And what ever happened to Jacobs, the saga-boy of form three? But I keep it to myself that Jacobs was the first boy to make me feel that way, that "first-sign-of-puberty-way", just by standing over me on a bus trip to an inter-college football match. But Jacobs wasn't in my class, he didn't sit in front of me, so it was Glen's back that I let my pen graze across, once, then twice. Glen's back that my finger brushed against. Glen's back that the white cotton moved against, while I enjoyed the sensation of his male flesh. I leave that unsaid too.

"Tell me about your wife," I say instead.

He takes a big swig from the flask and turns to me. "So you've heard the story about me, eh? Yuh want to know how it is that I end up living here instead of in a posh house like the rest of the boys from school. Or living the American dream like you?"

In the silent moment that follows I want to explain that that's not what I mean. I search for a way to explain that I'd left New York feeling out of control. Explain that I don't live the American dream, and I'm not sure what my own dreams are any more. But that's too much to try to say now.

"Nah man, nah. I'm just asking how you doing?"

"Maybe I should ask those other fellas how they've ended up living perfect little lives."

I reach over for the flask, which is wedged in the sand at his feet, touching his back with my other hand for balance. How is it that I have ended up here on this beach tonight?

"No, just tell me about your wife."

Glen tells me first that, yes she is his wife, even though some of the stories say they're just living together. He tells me that she's from Paramin, where they don't mix with outsiders. He met her the year after his parents died, within a month of each other. He tells me that they were married in a tiny little church because his family disapproved: his sister thought he was too young, it was too soon, his older brothers wanted him to meet a "proper" girl at university.

"That was when they still thought I was going to be just like one of them," he laughs.

He tells me that only his wife cuts his hair, no barber in the world can touch it. "But boy, you shoulda see the first time she put a scissors in my head. . . she *zug* up the thing so bad, I had to walk around with a cap for a week."

I think about how Leigh lets only his sister cornrow his hair. For the first time, I think about him with a calm, clear view – without the panic that set in after the accident and wouldn't leave. I take a big swig of the home-brew, and I take the time to feel the clean wet liquid in my mouth, feel the sharp burn as it spreads down my throat to my stomach. Inhaling slowly through my mouth, I savour the difference between the night air and my breath.

Glen tells me that now I have to meet his wife, since I've

heard so much about her, and oh yeah, the *babash* we're drinking is her uncle's recipe. Her uncle is the one who raised her – mother, father, friend. And his two brothers don't talk to him anymore, but they don't talk to each other either, except to fight over the family business. Fitting the parts together, he's told me how he has ended up living here, turning his back on the conflict, turning towards a different coast of the island and a new family – creating a new dream. I'm glad that I didn't run into Cole or Jacobs or one of our other classmates. Glen weaves a tapestry of his life, the same story that he knows people tell behind his back. The details are the ones his brothers sneer at, and that people in her village still whisper about. Details that in the telling from Paramin to Maracas to Phillip sound either crazy or like just a local joke. But Glen tells them with a simple pride – a calm contentment.

I'm outside this scene looking in. I'm looking at me sitting here, cradled in the rich, jade hills, swigging clear strong fire from the same bottle as this man, viewing his life through his own eyes and enjoying the moment. This is so close to a scene I have wished for, even imagined in lonely moments over the years. This scene has a different ending, but I laugh, happy with just the way it's been, not wanting more, not needing to be carried off on some other current.

"Let's walk back," I say.

"All right," he says, "and I'll stop talking about me and you can talk about you."

Yes, now I can talk about me. Soon enough I'll listen to my messages and answer my phone. But for right now, as we walk beside the surf, I'll tell Glen about how my apartment in

Brooklyn feels like home, and how the people at work sometimes remind me of the boys from school. I know that I'll wake
up tomorrow in a beach house on Maracas bay, not like a piece
of driftwood swept in on a rogue tide, but because I've decided
that this is my time to be here.

JUST NOW

In the south of Trinidad, a young man begins a trip from the office of his family's construction company. It's sunny and clear, and the young man – Glen Moore – will make his way in a big company truck easily up the Butler and Hochoy Highways, only slowing in traffic near the flood planes of County Caroni. In a few year's time this arable flatland will be transformed – rice paddies will be replaced by a patchwork of housing developments, sewn with homes from the affordable to the exclusive – but for now there is still sodden earth and sprouting green. And for now, Glen drives north and west, crablike. He skirts the busy streets of Port of Spain and then heads north again.

Sometimes, as a little boy, Glen sat in one of these big trucks as one employee or another of Moore Construction Ltd. drove over the island's bumpy roads. Glen's favourite driver, Mr. Jarvis, would speed up on a safe straightaway, lean hard when they rounded a wide turn and make screeching noises when he braked to a stop. It was the best adventure Glen could imagine, but those truck rides were really Glen's father's way of getting him to see the worksites. It was the Old Man's trick to ensure that the boy saw dirt and dust, back-hoes and wheelbarrows, bent backs and sweating brows

– to ensure that Glen knew what work looked like up-close. The Old Man had done the same with his other children, even with the girl, Gloria.

Today Glen will come in contact with more than just work. Today Glen – who has been lulled to sleep by breakers lapping on sand almost every day of his life – will travel into the northern hills, deep into "the bush" where light must curve around leaves to touch the ground. He will meet adults and children for whom gazing at the sea or playing on a sandy beach is an event, because, even on an island the size of Trinidad, there is a world of difference between life on the coast and life inland.

Glen's mother is excited about this trip. Marjory Moore didn't raise Glen to be the baby of the family, even though he is her youngest. Marjory – a woman who could find something worthwhile in almost anyone – found much to celebrate in the different wonders of each of her children as they grew. But she wasn't naive. "That same boy who come first in test," she would say with a small smile, "that boy, my son, is the one who I catch cuffing up his bigger brother"; or she would reply to someone admiring her daughter, "Yes thank you, my girl-child with the pretty-pretty plaits was not too long ago chasing a fowl under the house in her church clothes." She nurtured and took on the even bigger challenge of harnessing her children's wayward traits.

Now, though, they're all grown. Gregory and George are both married with children of their own, and they have firm reigns on the family business. Gloria, thriving as a single woman, is creating her own catering company. It is only Glen who hasn't yet found his path.

But now, from her view on the other side, Marjory can focus on her baby, enjoy his uniqueness just a bit more. Having a favourite child is a luxury afforded the dead.

In the hills where Glen will end up today, Cecelia Mendoza woke up at about the same time that Glen started his journey. Now, as she changes into the white outfit that she has been instructed to wear, raindrops form a beaded curtain on the windshield of Glen's truck. It is the rainy season, and mornings that begin with blue sky and sun, must be expected to turn to rain.

Nearly blinded by this rainfall, and unfamiliar with these roads, Glen winds his way up The Saddle – where opposing slopes rise and fall like a function in calculus. Maybe he should stop, but the narrow road doesn't leave much room for that, and Glen wants to get the truck to the site as promised. The engine drones in a low gear, the wheels turn steadily. Glen has a point to prove. He fought hard to be driving, instead of marching to his brothers' orders. His brothers disapprove of Glen doing this job, driving a truck. Glen's brothers take things too literally, they still believe that the Old Man ferried them out to construction sites to prepare them to run the business, to see the legacy up close. But Glen understands the more subtle meaning and he also knows how to get his way. Years of dealing with the Catholic Brothers at Presentation College taught him this – how an offer to set up labs for Brother Timothy got him out of the unending announcements and off-key hymns of morning assembly; how a spectacular goal during a football match saved him the extra practice laps. Glen is as clever as the Old Man, and as tenacious as Marjory. So for the past year, he has been hauling bricks, pouring cement and driving trucks – doing what he wants to – instead of working on a degree or at least training in the office. Glen drives on through the rain.

At the top of the hill, as Cecelia's uncle tucks a yellow orchid in her braided hair, the sun regains its sovereignty over the sky and the shower ends just as quickly as it began.

The fair sky brings Glen a sudden memory – he is kite flying with the Old Man, sailing a home-made "mad bull" way up high, and in a flash the wind drops, the string goes slack and the kite plummets fast. Now, Saut D'Eau Road draws him further into the stepped herb gardens of this village. He rocks in and out of rain-filled ruts, skirting muddy gutters. When he tries to turn in a broad flat yard, the tires of his truck sink into soft mud, and he is stuck. Glen is no longer on the planned route.

Two preschool boys in the yard across the street stop their play to watch the giant toy. Glen knows that trying to move the truck will only get it mired more deeply. His hand lingers on the gearshift for a moment, and then he shifts to park and turns off the ignition. The little boys try to make their young voices low like the engine as it turns over and dies. *Brrroogh.* Glen steps out and mud rises past the heel of his boots, threatens the hems of his coveralls. When he walks towards the nearest house, the threat is made real and dark mud splatters his legs.

"Well-well, that didn't take long at all," Tio Pedro says, watching from the kitchen window.

Cecelia – dressed in white, with a flower in her hair – watches from the front stairs.

Last night Cecelia walked through the forest. She picked

her way through thick mist that hid the leaves that grazed her arms and legs. Chilled by moist air against her naked body, she padded through wet dirt that forced its way between her toes at each step. One foot in front of the other, unguided and unsure of her direction, she walked until a group of lizards moved into her path. A dozen reptiles, a score – some as long as a forearm, others pinkie-small – brown ones and green ones, brown-and-green, rough and smooth – slithered in staggered, crooked lines, making patterns in the mud before her. Cecelia watched transfixed. She thought she recognized some pattern, some design, but always the creatures moved before she could fix any image in her mind.

One mottled lizard broke away from the troupe and began a fluid crawl, moving closer and closer to her. As she looked to escape, the wet, white haze about her took on a new form. Where, a moment before, Cecelia had seen the air billow and swirl as a single cloudy mass, she now sensed dozens of separate darting movements: a cloud of pale yellow butterflies flew off in every direction about her, moonlit wings soft against her skin.

The fluttering cleared and Cecelia looked down again. The rogue lizard had stopped inches before her feet. It angled its head, its eyes met Cecelia's, and it opened its mouth as though about to speak.

First thing in the morning, Cecelia went to Tio Pedro. Cecelia has never known the concern of a mother like Marjory, or even the guiding wings of older siblings. Cecelia's mother left this little village, running away from *country-bookie* ways and all the dusty old-people-business that held her brother Pedro in place. Cecelia's mother didn't have her brother's interest or his way of seeing. But in town, instead of modern office-work and suitors with sharply-creased trousers, Pedro's sister found menial labour and sweaty married men who rushed home to their wives. When she found herself pregnant, she came back to the village, back to her brother. She watched her brother between the groans of her labour, she watched him afterwards with the baby girl whose face was veiled in a bloody caul – watched him clean the child and bury the caul and the navel string, following the old *country-bookie* ways. Watched him in the days and weeks afterward, and saw enough to know that she wasn't needed again.

So it was Pedro to whom Cecelia turned for advice and comfort. It is only Pedro to whom she tells her dreams.

Today, Cecelia started her story, "First I was walking . . . just walking and walking."

She described her dream and Pedro listened carefully, translating each detail in his mind. When she reached the end – the almost talking lizard – Pedro sat quiet. In long moments, still, he bridges the gap between worlds and times. Pedro lives in a present filled with yesterday's ways and forgotten knowledge.

He began his instructions, "Go and boil up some sage-bush, yes?"

Cecelia nodded.

"Then after it boil good-good, when yuh see the colour change... take it off the fire and then add-in some *vertivier* leaf. Bathe yourself good in that essence water," Pedro said.

The herbs change from one time to the next – lime bud, *cousin majoe*, shining bush – sometimes they are added to bath water, sometimes they are steeped as tea, but always they soothe Cecelia, ground her. When she was a child, Pedro would make the baths himself or steep the tea and hold the cup as she drank. As she got older he began guiding her – standing over her as she pinched the leaves or stirred the water. Later he only instructed her, and left her to work independently. Some months ago, he began asking her questions, that led her to make her own decisions. "What lime bud does make yuh feel like? Yuh think de chandelier-bush will go good wit' what yuh see?" And so, on the last two or three occasions, Cecelia had told Tio Pedro not just the details of the dream, but she had also told him what bath she would prepare for herself, what leaves she would steep. He had nodded and smiled, and pulled down the flesh under his right eye.

This morning though, he had carefully given the instructions – taken control again – and Cecelia had been glad, because last night's dream was not like any she'd had before. Last night she had been more of a participant, less an observer. Last night felt intensely personal.

"When you finish, put on white clothes. Only white, you hear?" This part was new. "Make sure they don' have no other colour, yes. No little purple piping or red stripes or nothing so." Pedro had pulled down the flesh under his right eye – the familiar gesture that sealed agreement between dreamer and knower. But this morning Cecelia thought she'd seen something more in Tio's eye.

Pedro watches his niece walk off to follow his directive, pondering all that the day would bring her. Now, for the first time, Glen walks up to Pedro's house.

Cecelia, standing on the top of three steps, is a head above Glen. She stares at him, plainly, without guile. The separate features of his face – eyes, nose, lips – stand like hills formed on a single orb of dark stone. But the hems of his green coveralls are splattered, and he's flustered by being lost and stuck and late. All through his body there is the sense of arrested motion, of indecision. He looks like a caught animal.

He stares at her. She's not a pretty girl in any standard way – her eyes are disproportionately large for her head, her ears too prominent. Lanky legs jut from her white shorts. But her hair, plaited loose, forms a wavy frame around her face. Glen considers the whole image – curve, colour and light – and he remembers the day in art class when he was the only boy who thought the Picasso portrait Mrs. Baptiste showed them was beautiful. He remembers that hot Friday afternoon, remembers the way harsh angles blended into smooth arcs, remembers wishing that he could see the real canvas, the way the paint lay on it. He remembers not caring about the *fatigue,* the pointed teasing from his classmates: "That is why Moore eh have no girlfriend, he waiting fuh a *choonks* with two eye on the same side of she head."

Now, two little boys cross the street to examine the truck; to them it is beautiful. Pedro examines his niece and the stranger.

"Mister, what yuh watching me so for?" Cecelia flashes her teeth, playful. "Like yuh expect me to move your truck for yuh."

"Move my truck, Miss?" Glen joins in the game, quick. "What make you feel that right there in that spot is not exactly where I want that truck to be."

"Oh-ho. You wake up this morning and decide to drive all the way up here, and park in my Uncle yard?"

"Nah, hear what happen, eh?" Glen places one booted foot

on the first step, slips a hand in his pocket. "I was going and spend the day by the beach, play some football and thing, but this fella come and tell me that if I drive up here I could see the nicest woman in Trinidad."

"And is what? Yuh want me to help you look for she?"

"Nah, don't try that trick, girl." Glen says. "The fella tell me to find the girl with a yellow flower in her hair."

"Oh, well wait 'til I see that man," she says, "I tired tell him to stop sending just any and everybody up here to me."

"Well, in truth, people don't usually call me 'Anybody', or 'Everybody' for that matter," he says. "People does call me Glen."

"Well right now, I think I should call you Muddy."

"Alright you could call me that, but then don' get vex when I make up a name for you."

"Before you start calling people names, better remember you is the one with the truck trap in the mud."

The two stand playing and laughing for a while. The boys are playing around the truck, feeling the heat of the engine, measuring themselves against the huge tyres. The steel creature is, to them, far more interesting than the timeworn banter between a young man and a young woman. But Marjory is interested; she likes this girl who's strong enough to make her son work, funny enough to make him laugh. And Pedro is interested. This is his niece, this is future.

Pedro examines Glen's height and size, the way he stands and how his eyes move when he talks. Examines the way his niece responds. To unknowing eyes this would seem a casual conversation. But Pedro sees brightness around his niece's face, sees how she seems to cleave into Glen, how his body

curves around hers. So Pedro, no casual observer, sees the
changing, the leaving. Present in this moment, Pedro breathes
a fading past and sees a deepening future. Pedro sees Pedro
standing alone.

Pedro is not a selfish man. He spent his life tending to ways
that have lost value, worked nights with those who didn't want
him near – a lifetime misunderstood – but at this stage he feels
unready to let go, unprepared for this change.

So, as much as Pedro considers Glen and Cecelia, he is
considering himself – his own fears and worries, the things he
has done, things left undone. He looks at them now, and he
rehashes the past and contemplates the future. If Cecelia were
to look at him, just now, she would see for certain that there
is "something more" in his eyes. But she is still looking at
Glen.

I want to see him closer, Pedro thinks.

Glen remembers that he is supposed to be at the construction site, not standing with this girl-woman in a muddy yard
in this small village.

"Yuh know, I was supposed to be in Santa Cruz ages ago."

"The tune change already?" Cecelia says. "Yuh well forget
about the man and the yellow flower, fast."

"I forget that man, yes," Glen says. "But not the flower."

"Oh gosh, Mister, come get your muddy ol' truck out of we
yard."

Cecelia turns to the door. She walks – long legs poking
through white shorts, a plain white T-shirt falling loosely to
her high backside. It's stark white against the sunny reds of her
skin, highlighted by the yellow flower at the base of the single
plait running down her neck.

Pedro recognizes that this is the same girl who came home from standard two crying, "Tio, the girls in school... in meh class... the girls call me 'horse face'." He told her the usual things that day. "Don' bother with them, they too blind and *stupidy* to see how pretty yuh is." He told her, too, how beautiful horses are. Graceful. That little girl with tears running down her face. This same woman, walking forward with careless poise. Glen watching and learning behind her; Pedro waiting and knowing ahead.

In Pedro's kitchen, Cecelia says, "This is my uncle, Pedro Mendoza, people does call him Tio. Tio, this man was trying to swim in the yard."

"Good morning. . ." Glen hesitates, not sure if he qualifies as "people", or if he should use Mr. Mendoza.

Pedro doesn't give him time to decide, "So you float in here on the rain cloud and feel you could stand boldface in my yard, chatting-up my niece just so?"

No smiles, no extended hands. Just three people in a small room, looking at each other. The wooden walls are unpainted, decorated chiefly with scattered knot holes. The only accessories are white: bleached cotton hangs from a clothesline at the window; plastic, stamped with a lace pattern, covers the table; and in one corner a trinity of partially burned, milky candles have dripped waxy stalactites.

"Well, Mr. Mendoza, sorry, I jus'. . ." Glen's apology floats unfinished as he looks at Pedro. For a minute he tries to connect this face to Cecelia's. But Pedro's firmly-set mouth, bordered by deep folds of tamarind-pod skin, is too far from Cecelia's simple smiles – the smiles that made him lose track of time.

"I really have to leave. . . I have to go to Santa Cruz."

"Leave? Look boy, you ain' going nowhere right this minute." Pedro looks at his niece, and tugs at the flesh under his right eye.

Perhaps Glen should be bothered by Pedro's statement. Maybe he should be trying to figure out what Pedro's gesture to his niece signifies. But Glen is captivated by the hand itself, more than by the movement of the hand. He follows it in an arc from hip to face and back to hip. He looks at its mirror. Two hands. Hands of an old man, but not so old, maybe the age of Glen's Old Man if he were alive. Hands of a man who has known work, no harder or easier than the workers on the construction sites. But these hands are different – skin so dark it seems to trap all light near it, creased and cragged. Creviced more than they are wrinkled. Deep lines, not at the knuckles and fingers as they should be, but higher toward the wrist. Skin that looks more like bark than an old man's flesh.

Cecelia knows the hands, so it's the movement that she takes note of. She should be reassured by Pedro's gesture – their familiar sign of concord – but for the first time it seems like a signal of exclusion rather than of a comforting bond. Cecelia doesn't want Pedro to exclude Glen. She doesn't expect him to. She is used to seeing Pedro welcome and nurture, enfold and succour. For the first time, she sees her uncle as this other being, the figure whom the children at school whispered about as they stood apart from her. "Don' get she vex, Pedro is she uncle, he could. . . My mother say don' even talk to she, she family does. . ."

"The rain coming again," Pedro says. His gaze is not

towards the sky, but aimed at Glen, steady. "Don' worry, we go take care of you."

Glen looks to Cecelia for help in getting out of this compelling invitation, and realizes in this instant that he's already considering this girl-woman as an ally. But before she can take a side, before Glen can continue his protest, the rain bursts forth again.

"Yuh see," Pedro says. "So just have some sitting down."

Glen sits at the kitchen table with Cecelia. Pedro stands. Hovers. His awareness of what this day is for his niece does not calm him. Knowing does not mean accepting. Marjory knows and Marjory is calm. Accepting is another luxury granted the dead.

"Mr. Moore, I know yuh eh used to country-bookie ways like ours," Pedro says. "But make yuhself comfortable."

And as if to make that very instruction impossible, as if to scare away any hope of comfort, Pedro goes on, "I cyah understand how the driver of a fancy-fancy truck could end up stick in my yard. Like you thief the truck? Or yuh thief yuh license? Which one?"

"Oh gosh Tio, yuh go frighten the man," Cecelia says. Her eyes avoid Glen's now, even when she says, "Don' study him nah, he playing."

Cecelia is wrong, Pedro is not just playing.

Glen, feeling Pedro's eyes boring into him, believes he is being judged. Glen is wrong, too. Pedro is staring at Glen but not judging him. He is not really looking at Glen, as much as he is looking at the future. Looking at the past. Looking at himself.

Pedro sees himself not though Glen's eyes or through

his own, but through Cecelia's. He knows that she is surprised to see him act like this with a stranger: gruff, closed, enigmatic. Cecelia who knows Pedro better than anyone living today. But all that he knows, all that he sees, is overridden by all that he feels. Washed away by the questions: *How it is that my niece get so big? So grown and ready to move on? How it is that I eh teach her everything I supposed to? Is fail, I fail?* The worry, the creeping loneliness, the sense of failure. He excuses himself and walks into the other room.

Glen wonders what Pedro is doing there. He suspects that Pedro is eavesdropping, judging, but he is wrong again. Glen doesn't know that Pedro stands staring out the window, tracing drops of rain as they fall from a single leaf at the end of a spindly, curved branch. Watching water appear, bead, roll and fall. Again and again. Hundreds of times, an action repeated on ever leaf on that pommerac tree. Repeated on every leaf of every tree in this yard, under this rain cloud. Who but Pedro would see down to one drop at a time? Who else but Pedro or Marjory? Who but the ancient or the dead?

And when the rain slows, and lets up, when the sun throws rays of light, instead of droplets of water on that solitary leaf, Pedro sees the light and the water on the leaf at the same time. Recognizes that it is all together his *now* – the sunlight, the rainwater, the leaf. The baby with the caul, the girl coming home in tears from school, the woman with the yellow flower in her hair. But Glen won't know when Pedro knows. Marjory knew it before.

When Pedro returns, Cecelia and Glen are talking as before. What Pedro overhears is Glen saying, "...used to say that the best part of her married life was when they were living in a little shack."

"You never live in no shack, your hand too smooth," Cecelia says.

"I never live in the shack but I used to play in it all the time. That shack still standing up. But when my mother used to say that – about how nice life was in the shack – the Old Man used to *stewps*, suck his teeth and say, 'Woman don't talk foolishness'. But I know it was true, I could look at his face and see his eyes watching my mother, happy."

"So, one day yuh go take some lucky girl and make she live in a shack?"

Glen laughs, "A lucky, lucky girl."

Pedro sets a bowl of plums between them. "Don' go back down the hill and say that people up here didn't even offer yuh something to eat," he says.

The fruit run the spectrum from unripe to ripe: they form a polka-dotted heap of dark-green, yellow-green and golden-yellow. Once again Glen looks to Cecelia, this time for reassurance or a cue. Then he considers the folly of this. Glen, like every eligible man on this island, knows that it's risky to eat from someone you don't know, from someone who might wish to trap you. Perhaps not so much knows, as has heard jokes about "stay home" in the sweet bread, or "sweat rice" that made big-big men lose their power. But Glen looks at the bowl of fruit, looks at Cecelia and laughs to himself. He reaches out and picks up a plum.

As he does, he feels Pedro's eyes on him. Glen hands the plum to Cecelia. She knows about the country tales too, and she knows they have crossed Glen's mind. She laughs out loud. As she laughs, Glen takes another plum and together they take bites of the fruit. Pedro watches. In years to come – after separate days of blue skies and sun, after rainy seasons and dry seasons, after the rice paddies of County Caroni have been replaced by housing developments – Glen will tell the story. He will say, "I tell myself, what 'stay home' she could put on that food that could have me any more catch? I say, if she could make me more tie down to she, I want that. Just so." And when Glen tells this story, Cecelia will laugh and her eyes will look like the Old Man's when Marjory talked about the shack.

For now, Cecelia plucks the ripest plums, savouring the sweet, juicy pulp. She tells Glen about playing high in the hills under the stars. Glen favours the tart green plums. He talks about mornings on the beach and about the only meal his father ever cooked.

They talk of football and fruit, and of time and tides. Glen will get his truck out of the mud, and he will drive off as two little boys imitate the truck's engine, *vroom*. Looking at the road ahead, he will see in the rear view mirror, in the corner of his eye, he will see Cecelia standing with Pedro. Pedro with his ancient hand on his niece's shoulder will be saying, "Don' worry, he coming back soon. You go see him just now."

MARJORY'S MEAL

No one noticed the Old Man during that last week. The first day, he had just started getting everything ready, not fully decided on what he would do. In the old shed that still stood in the patch of trees at the bottom of the hill, he started sweeping with the home-made *cocoyea* broom that stood in the corner. Though everyone now called it the old shed, not so long ago it seemed, it had been their daughter Gloria's dolly house for tea parties. Before that, the big fort for the older boys' war games. Only Glen, the youngest, had not spent much time there. But in the beginning, it had been the marriage house – the place where the Old Man had proudly brought Marjory, his then new wife. And though now it was seldom used, he had been drawn there, maybe for the memories, maybe for some solitude in which to find calm. As he swept the dust and cobwebs away, he could hear her laugh, a mix of shyness, fear, hope and happiness. When they had lived in this wooden shack, he had promised her that the world and their lives together lay just ahead, simply awaiting their grasp. Now, all these years later, it would be the right place for him to prepare this thing, this delicate meal.

In the dewy hours of Tuesday, he had moved through the kitchen in the main house deciding what he could take to the shed, while Gloria was still asleep. Not because he needed to sneak around or act like a thief in his own home, but rather because this preparation was so fragile in his mind, and so personal a labour, that he felt the need to hold it close to him, and so to keep it just for him and Marjory. He selected some enamel plates and bowls from the set that no one used any more, tucked away back in the cabinet near the kitchen table; from the cupboard over the kitchen sink, he took the old grater that looked like a percussion instrument and hadn't been used since the shiny, stainless-steel Osterizer had taken its place; took some wooden spoons and a beat-up wood-handled knife from the back of one of the drawers; and finally, the stone mortar and pestle from on top of the cupboard. The Old Man hadn't climbed up this high in a long time. No one used this old-fashioned grinding tool any more, but it still sat atop the cupboard like a simple sculpture on display; it was the one thing that might be missed.

At 11 o'clock he sat on a stool in the back of the shed, facing the woods with an orange and the wood-handled knife in his lap. He could just hear the waves lapping on shore, singing a harmony to the melody of the rustling leaves, broken by the rhythm of a loud bird asking over and over *"Qu'est que il dit, keskidee"*. Absent-mindedly he worked at the orange, slipping the sharp blade between the rind and the fleshy white pith, not noticing the mini-explosions of fragrant oil sparking on his hands. He focused instead on making an inventory and on planning the rest of the week, planning the meal. Eventually he looked down and saw that he'd created a single, long spiral of orange rind. When the children were still young, he would peel an orange or a grapefruit like this, keeping the rind in one long, curvy snake – a father's simple magic act to entertain them. But they were not here now, so he just wiped the knife's blade on his old pants and then cut the orange in two along its equator. He sucked the orange with the sweet juices running down his chin, mixing with his salty sweat and saliva, like the jumble of emotions swirling in his heart. He hung the orange rind on a nail-head to dry, the first ingredient of the meal.

He hadn't, though, started to plan what he would cook. Marjory had no appetite, and when she did eat, it was hard for her to keep anything down. So though he had formed the idea of the meal, he was still unsure of what it would be. But the one thing that was unquestionable was that there would be blue crab. Some way, it had to have blue crab in there.

The first frugal meal Marjory had cooked for them, the day after they had gotten married, was blue crab, curried crab. They had been awkward around each other, and the marriage dance that they would eventually master was still a tentative two-step, with neither of them quite sure where the hands went or how to shift on a downbeat. So he had gone out that day, as much to settle his soul, and to ground himself in the natural world of the coast and the mangrove, as to bring back some specific item. Nonetheless, he had ended up coming back home with half a dozen blue crabs he had caught. Marjory had cleaned them, seasoned them and curried them down – a dry, smoky curry made over the coal pot.

They ate quietly in the simple shack that would be theirs until years later when he built the house up the hill. The kerosene lamp on the bare wooden table between them cast their silhouettes in two grand, flickering shadows on the walls.

The crab was good, and they cracked into the shells and sucked out the sweet meat, licking the brown-yellow sauce off their fingers. Right after that meal of curried crab, they were together for the first time as a man and woman. Yes, they had spent the previous night in the same bed, but unlike an American movie, or an English romance novel, that honeymoon night had been strange and shy and their marriage had remained unconsummated.

It was on the second night that they had flowed with the currents that pulled them towards each other. On that second night, with all the manly strength that he felt – the power that he had used with abandon on a handful of other women before they were married – he had taken his place as her husband over her. And on the same night she had shown her simple, earthy majesty over him. Yes, lying under him, she held on to the taut skin at his hipbones as he felt all of his hardness inside her. It was like this, almost always like this, that she would guide him as they were joined in love. She would hold on and he would be moved – grinding, riding – to her unspoken direction; she would touch him there and push back when she was ready, raise up to meet his thrust, then pull him back down slowly and wind in surging, assured circles; eventually she would grab the back of his neck, drawing his face to her hot bosom, raising their passion to a climax. Anyone watching might have seen only the strong, sweating husband and believed that he was in control, like watching a boat on the water with no awareness of the rudder underneath, pushing the tide to make the hull turn this way or that.

By Wednesday he started gathering more ingredients. He would need a good pumpkin – nothing big, but one sweet and full of perfume. He didn't have to worry much about picking the right one because the pumpkin vine in the back of the main house was always bearing and it never had a bad gourd on it. While he was back there, he was drawn to the pumpkin blossoms like a bee seeking pollen. So when he returned to the shed, his haul was not just a ripe, fragrant pumpkin, but also some delicate pumpkin flowers that he couldn't seem to leave behind. To this harvest bouquet, he added a bunch of limes and a handful of lime buds.

On Thursday he would get the other ingredients. He would put on long, rubber boots, walk half a mile north along the shore, and then into the mangrove to catch crab. He would bring back four hairy, blue crabs, so that he could select the best ones when he cooked. From one of the coconut trees on the way back he would pick a few coconuts – insurance again, so that by Friday he would have the right one to grate, not so green that the flesh inside was still a jelly, but not so old that the coarse copra was spoiled and rancid. "Always make sure yuh keep some options on the table", he had cautioned his boys about business through the years. But truth be told, that was a lesson he'd learned, as a boy, from watching his own mother manage her house.

Not one of the four children that Marjory had given him saw that he was up to something during that week. They talked to him – "Daddy, come and eat something. Yuh have to eat." And they talked about him – "George, how you think the Old Man making out with this thing?" But each one of the children was busy with the jobs they had found for themselves or that the others had assigned them. Gloria was the chief nurse and ever at their mother's side. Gregory focused on the business, keeping all the daily problems to himself and sparing the others petty worry. George organized doctors' visits, and medicine deliveries and made arrangements with the priest and church elders. Glen, still in school at Presentation, had been ordered to keep his mind on his upcoming exams. The one thing that the Old Man had preached and preached over the years, one thing that they had all learned, was that regardless of the undertaking, you were supposed to perform well. And maybe they had all learned this lesson because of his painterly tales about working in the coconut groves as a boy, and in the oil field in his youth or building the business as a man – tales he told again and again. Or maybe even because of the *cut-tails* they used to get if they shirked their chores when they were growing up, or because, each day, the Old Man showed them by example in the work he did himself. But maybe, too, they got it without him knowing, without them knowing, from being in the house with Marjory.

Marjory had been the Old Man's life. The world might never have known it. The church people in the little Point Cocoa Anglican Church and the wives of business associates who came to the compound for the annual New Year's Day party might have seen only the lucky country girl whose husband had built a big-time business and put her and her children in a nice house on the hill. But the Old Man always knew it, because it was the wellspring of his strength and the light of his purpose. While the great poets had their muses to inspire their works, to fuel their creativity, Marjory had inspired his whole life and been his whole, quiet passion.

Gloria and George, the older two, had grown up in the lean years before the money. They had seen their mother spend as much time and invest as much care in preparing lunch when she had only a few green figs and some yams, as when she had chickens to bake and cheese and milk enough to make macaroni pies. Gregory had seen her iron his school uniform every night to make sure the crease lasted all day long. Glen had seen her crochet the tablecloth that they still used at Easter and Christmas, and the antimacassars for the chair arms, and even the cloth that was used on the altar when the Bishop visited their church.

On Friday, while he could still hear the gravel crunch under the jeep's tyres as the boys left for the day, he got dressed. He walked down the hill as the first light sparkled off the moist crystals on the grass. As usual, he was glad for the early morning stillness, a quiet that could only be had before the soft lap of low-tide waves was broken by the cock's crow. This same soft light and gentle sound had allowed him as a little boy to dream big dreams; as a young man to plot grand schemes; as a man to plan his moves before the day's challenges; and now, as an old man, to remember, and to think simple, peaceful thoughts. This last week, there had been no big dreams or wild schemes, only a rising tide of memory as he moved with purpose and strength, powered by the pull of some distant moon.

Again he sat down with an orange and the wood-handled knife. For five days now he had been working on this, working for the first time not on what he wanted, not towards a chosen destination, but simply accepting what seemed like the only choice that life was allowing. For a lifetime he had created his own paths, slashing through thickets of what often seemed

like the island's indigenous barriers – poverty, classism, jealousy, corruption – and still made his own way. With that same
drive, for the past months he had fought against accepting any
of this. He'd fought and slashed, planned and imagined, all up
until this last week. But this week had brought an acceptance of
Marjory's condition. After his initial denial, then growing anger
and even more powerless frustration, finally he was swimming
with the rip-tide instead of fighting against it. Now he sat with
the juice of the orange running down his chin, juice suddenly
matched by salty tears flowing from a deep well of loss, pushed
to the calm surface of what had been his pool of strength. The
tears came drop by drop, pooling until they flowed, and flowing
more and more until they bloomed into sound – one low, deep
sob and then another and another, until his body was shaking.
Then he had to set the knife down as he crumbled from his
middle, folding at the gut and catching his head in his hands.
There, with the breeze still gently stirring the leaves, with the
birds still singing sweetly and the waves still lapping on the
shore, he cried alone.

Down in the shed, the Old Man started his Marjory's Meal.

Ingredients:
2 blue crabs
2 cups of coconut milk
1 cup of pumpkin, roasted & crushed
2 pumpkin blossoms
1 lime
several lime 'buds'
dried peel of 1 orange

spice sticks (cinnamon)
pinch of salt
2 teaspoons of brown sugar

Coconut milk

Husk and break open dried coconut with cutlass or machete; drain liquid and reserve to drink later; remove coconut meat from shell; grate coconut meat to a fine pulp over bowl; add enough water to make pulp moist but not runny; in a clean, cotton cloth, twisted into a closed bulb, squeeze moist pulp in batches over a bowl until it yields no more milk.

Roasted pumpkin

Place a large wedge of ripe pumpkin, skin side down, in the white coals of a coal pot; roast until flesh of pumpkin is tender to a fork (about ½ hour); remove from coals and let it cool to touch; scoop flesh from pumpkin skin and place in mortar; grind with pestle to a coarse puree.

Orange Peel tea

Bring two cups of water to a rapid boil, add about four or five inches of dried orange peel to water and let steep for at least five minutes; remove peel and serve in teacups sweetened with one teaspoon of brown sugar per cup.

Pumpkin blossoms stuffed with crabmeat

Clean crabs thoroughly – remove backs and any sand or mud. Rinse under running water and rub liberally with lime.

Place coconut milk in cast iron pot on a rack over the coal pot.

Add lime buds, a spice stick and remaining orange peel and bring to a gentle boil.

Add crabs and simmer until cooked – about 15 minutes.

Remove crabs from pot and let cool to touch.

Crack crab and remove crabmeat from shell.

Combine crabmeat with pumpkin; season lightly with salt, adding just enough of reserved coconut boiling liquid to achieve a creamy texture.

Gently stuff mixture into pumpkin blossoms with a spoon, leaving enough room to twist flower closed.

Place stuffed pumpkin blossoms on coconut shells and roast briefly over coals, about 5 minutes.

Arrange stuffed blossoms on plates and decorate with lime buds and spice sticks.

Serve with orange peel tea.

Down in the shed the Old Man started his mission by lighting the coal pot. The coals would burn, heating to the right temperature while he saw to the other preparations. Outside, he smashed the coconut open, then absorbed himself in transforming the rough white and brown flesh, first into a coarse, speckled meal, then a soft mush, and finally into a creamy white liquid. He cut the pumpkin, scraping away the tangled mesh of seeds, and put a wedge of it into the coal pot's "oven". Then he moved the stone off the wire-mesh covering and pulled the two best crabs still clawing from the pail. Cleaning them, he thought about Marjory's curry, but knew that the lightly spiced, softly perfumed approach he planned was right, for as he finished the meal, taking time with each specific step, he infused the process with a little of all that he had gotten from his Marjory over the years.

When he was done, he walked back up the hill and climbed the back stairs into the kitchen; there he placed the covered tray on the table, and when he told Gloria to go into town, the finality of the statement didn't leave room for her to question, or protest that she had to stay and take care of her mother.

"Take the car and go to Point and get some stamps and envelopes," he said. But he touched her arm before she walked out the door and said, "Don't worry, I can take care of your mother."

The Old Man stands with the tray at the bedroom doorway watching Marjory propped up on the pillows. Tentative, suddenly, he remembers the postures of their children bringing their first report-card home, he sees Gloria standing before him with a Father's day card made in school and Glen with a "mad bull" kite that he wanted help to fly. Marjory turns ever so slightly, a shift of her head to the left, enough for him to see that she is awake, but with enough tightness in her jaw to betray the effort this small move takes.

"Marge," he says softly. "Marjory, I brought you a little something to eat."

Moving more quickly now, he goes over to the bed, placing the tray on the side table, and then moves a chair so he can sit beside her.

"Come and eat a little bit of this, girl," he says as he moves the dish-towel away to show the tray. The pastel pumpkin blossoms and spice-sticks balance the deep green of the lime buds on the plate.

"But ay-ay," she says softly. "What is all this, pretty, pretty flowers and spice?"

"Well you know I ain' no cook, but I tried to make a little thing here," he says, matching her small smile. "Just for the two of us, okay?"

He cuts into one of the flowers, and holds the lightly loaded fork to her lips. Then, taking a forkful for himself, he is comforted that the pumpkin is easy to chew, happy that the whole work is moist, sweet, and delicate.

"Here Marge, drink some orange peel tea," he says. Wordless, accompanied by the sounds of the breeze though the trees, they continue these steps: a small fork for her, a fork for him, a sip of tea.

As they make their way past the halfway mark, she looks at him and says, "Crab, eh? Boy, you remember to put crab in here too," with a trace of the sparkle that has kept him happy for so many years.

After they have eaten together, they sit quietly in the afternoon light, the Old Man seated in the straight-backed mahogany chair, his Marjory nestled on the soft mattress. He doesn't hear the sea moan down the hill; after a lifetime of its company, it's like the sound of his own breathing. As he has done on so many nights for their lifetime together, now he absorbs the rhythm of his wife's breathing, even this low, laboured cadence – and that too, he does not hear.

In this quiet, for the first time since he has know this woman who has brought him so much, he feels that he has given her a real gift. Almost forty years ago, he had brought her a cheap scent, essence of lavender, that he'd awkwardly chosen to try to win her attention. At the time, he'd thought that the feeling of inadequacy had come because he had wanted to buy something more expensive, something grander. But through the years, as they grew together, as his pockets deepened and his options increased, the feeling returned. Fancy linen hand-kerchiefs, gold bangles and chains, and real French perfume. But still the feeling – over and over again – until he recognized the reality that she had given him more than he could ever match.

And now, though it is not the case that he feels a balance of the scales, he watches her drift gently into sleep and feels that he has given her something small and meaningful. It will be this moment, this gift, that he will clutch to his heart when he drifts into his own final sleep that will take him to meet her once more, just months after she leaves him, sitting on a wooden chair, in a gentle breeze, in their house on the hill.

HOW FAR, HOW LONG

As the Chinatown Express rolls past New Calvary Cemetery, Ray knows that he's hooked. More than three hours, and one short rest stop, after leaving Boston, this cemetery should only signal that home is close, the Midtown Tunnel near, the steepled skyline in the background.

Ray's passed this stretch of highway before. Snaking along the BQE on his way back from LaGuardia or peeling off the LIE coming home from random dates deep in Queens, heading back from the beach in Long Island. But today, this afternoon, staring out through the large-framed window, Ray looks at fresh-cut lawn and thinks that it looks pile-carpet plush. Granite headstones of irregular heights and sizes, square-cut and round-edged, sit like gems on a jeweller's tray. The sun casts opalescent patches between the leaves. Angel statues seem frozen in flight, stone wings caught mid-flutter.

Ray usually avoids cemeteries, plans an alternate route, buries his head in a magazine, forces his mind to go blank. Anything but think, anything but remember. But right now he's captured, captivated. Happy. He imagines different lives for each plot, individual stories of friends and work, pictures of homes and picnics, tales of lovers' quarrels and tender make-ups. Life in place of death, connection instead of loneliness. So yeah, he knows that he's hooked. Gotta be "hooked" though, 'cause Ray won't use the l-word, but hooked sure as a catfish on a nylon line.

When the bus stops on Christie Street in Manhattan, Ray is one of the first passengers to walk out into the Chinatown air. He walks along Canal Street, through the tourists and bargain hunters, past the vendors and fruit stands, down the subway steps, and just makes it onto a Q-Express as the doors close. The train snakes into the tunnel and up onto the Manhattan Bridge. The skyline – unseen behind him, yet so familiar – forms a kind of decompression chamber from Boston to Brooklyn. Without looking, Ray knows the sights. Tenements crowded together, give way to high-rise projects as if in surrender. The snaking boundary of FDR highway that's always traffic-littered. After that come the downtown towers, a few old stone faces rising noble between steel-and-glass-framed youngsters. And of course, the space where The Towers used to reign, where, for many, the phantoms will always stand.

On Ray's right, a tow-headed boy in a Yankee's cap sits next to his father. The kid's face is bright and open as he stares out the window. But the man looks uncomfortable, confused. His chino-and-topsider style marks him as a tourist.

The tourist pulls out a subway map, not standard MTA issue; it's small and nicely bound. Attractive and probably useless. The boy, about four or five, leans over to look at the map, the brim of his cap poking the man's arm.

"Are we going the right way, Daddy?" Kid probably understands the map as well as the man.

"Well, let's see." The man looks up at Ray, then looks quickly away. An old lady in black Oxford shoes cleans a spot on her glasses. A teenage Asian couple share the ear-pods of an MP3 player. Dad turns back to the map. Then looks up at Ray again, taking in his cap, stud-earrings, hip-hop-label gear.

"Does this train go to midtown?"

"Uh-uh. Brooklyn."

The tourist's forehead furrows. "Brooklyn."

Ray says, "You can just get off at the next stop and take a train headed back the other way." Lucky thing he's in such a good mood, he wouldn't volunteer this much info on a regular day.

"What, Daddy?"

"We're just going for a little trip. Look over there. See?" the man says. "There's another bridge."

Soon, Brooklyn buildings fill the windows. Maybe too soon. Travel always makes Ray feel good and a good trip always seems done too soon. Too soon the Q-train spans the bridge, and dives into the tunnel. Too soon it pulls into DeKalb station. Ray points the tourist father and son toward the right train and heads upstairs to the street.

★

The weekend in Boston had been nice – but just that – fun, nice, not spectacular. But Julian had been spectacular. On Saturday when Julian met Ray's bus, he stood out from a mismatched little crowd – taller, more stylish, handsome. His sun-brushed dreadlocks fell onto a linen shirt that surfed on waves of muscle. A funky belt buckle, Indian bracelets, blue jeans. But his best accessories were his laid-back manner and his small smile – that hinted at larger ones to come.

"A'ight Beantown, here I am."

"And all Boston cheers. . . Glad you made it through the rain okay."

"Yo. Wasn't so sure I was okay, 'til I saw your cute, cheesy smile."

"Yeah? Well you know, once I saw that cap on the bus, turned backwards. . . I knew it was you, and I just smiled." Julian smiled wider.

A short walk and a train-ride later and Ray was strolling through a quaint, hilly neighbourhood with Julian pointing out his favourite spots: the bakery where both the grand-mother and the grandson flirt with him; the pizza place where slices come with double pepperoni; the cleaners where the owner calls him "Jamaica". Up a steep hill and a short flight of stairs, and they walked into Julian's first-floor apartment.

They stayed in all that night. Julian made dinner – chopping, sautéing, stirring – while Ray flipped through a scrapbook with clippings and photos from Julian's performances as a dancer and a choreographer. Neither talked much. Occasional com-ments about the mementos – "These shots are great, the camera loves you, man". Questions about the food – "You like mush-rooms?. . . Not allergic to hazelnuts are you?" But accompanied by the melody of sizzling veggies and the rhythm of knife against chopping board, the room filled with a spice-like inti-macy, and fragrant trails of herbs circled about them.

★

The Con-Ed construction project is still under way, orange plastic barrels lined up at the corner. A gust swirls pieces of litter and takes hold of yellow "caution" tape, billows it in a high arc like a monochrome rainbow. By the time Ray's walked the eight blocks between the subway and his apartment he feels that he's seen as many people here as he did all weekend in Boston.

Inside, Ray thinks that his studio looks smaller, drab. For the first time, he thinks that maybe he should decorate it a bit – a couple pictures here and there, some colour. Julian's place was catalogue-photograph nice. Boy's a dancer, but he could make a real living styling folks' homes. Thing about Julian that scored him points though, wasn't that his place was gorgeous – sleek and intimate, funky and warm – no the thing is Julian didn't make a big deal about it, no attitude, no boasting. Definite points for that.

And of course his place seems smaller. He's spent the last few hours gazing at late-spring woods and suburban hills through a moving picture frame.

He drops his bag, unzips it and starts to unpack. Toiletries in the bathroom. Dirty socks and underwear make it to the laundry bag. Then, right there, between the shirts that he hadn't worn, is a gift bag, blue tissue paper poking out. "Boy's got moves," Ray says, aloud to the empty room. The tissue smells like Julian, like Julian's apartment – sage, shea butter, myrrh. Inside, a carved wooden paperweight, an elephant trumpeting in bas relief inside a circle of flowers.

Ray scans his apartment, settles on his makeshift coffee table, and places Julian's gift atop the fashion magazines in the centre.

When he picks up the phone, he should be dialling Julian's number. In fact Ray would swear that he planned to call, say thanks for the weekend, for the present. But he doesn't make that call, and on the third ring it's Ezra who answers.

"Ez-rah." Ray makes the last syllable sound like a deity as he summons an image of Ezra – Latino shading and fine, sharp features that suggest Egypt's confluences.

"Ray," Ezra says. "What's Ray-ly good, son?"

The two don't know each other that well, but this little name game started the night they met. And Ezra is smooth, always ready with slick lines, able to make them flow. Ray likes that, but right now he cuts through the wordplay.

"Where you at?" he says.

"Gym. . . Just about to hit the shower and be out," Ezra says.

"So you in my 'hood," Ray says. "Then swing through, yo."

"You want me to *swing through*? For real?"

"For real."

"A'ight. . . Lemme clean off alla this sweat and I'll. . ."

"Forget that. I got a shower," Ray breaks in. "Run over, get sweatier. I want you nasty."

Ray had never spent more than a couple of minutes on the phone with Ezra. No conversations, even as glib as Ezra was. Quick banter and direct to the point. But with Julian, minutes slipped into hours on the phone. He'd met Julian and Ezra within two days of each other. He danced with Julian at the club, liked the closeness of Julian's brawn, liked it even more when Julian sought him out in the crowd to say good night. Since then they'd talked for hours and hours on the phone. Julian poetic, Julian philosophic, Julian romantic. Julian said that he thought that Ray "needed a hug" when he first saw him. Said that he'd known him a long time ago. Past lives and all that kinda thing, but he made it sound sensible, sweet, tender. Julian played him vintage Stevie Wonder and sang the words to "Ribbon in the Sky".

He had this knack for looking at things in ways that Ray couldn't. Like the couple at the waterfront.

They only left Julian's apartment once during the weekend. Sunday, after a huge early breakfast with omelettes and fruit, coffee and toast, they went down to Boston Harbor. The day was grey and overcast and they stood quiet and almost alone, tides of warm moist air from Julian's mouth lapping against Ray's cheeks.

A middle-aged man walked up behind them, and when they turned he asked them to take a picture of him and the woman on his arm. To Ray, the white man looked like some ex-biker gone soft around the middle, and the woman's dark roots showed through a frizzy perm. But Julian didn't seem to mind the intrusion. He smiled and took the camera, set the shot carefully.

After the photo, instead of leaving, the man started talking. "...That was twelve years ago... This lady right here... twelve years today. . . she said yes. . ."

The couple finally walked away, and Ray was about to make a snide comment, when Julian said, "That was magical."

Ray couldn't stop the "Huh?" that came out.

"Twelve years together – cool. And, they chose us to take their picture today. It's like a visitation. Like angels wishing us well."

Like that – so strange – a viewpoint so different from what Ray was used to. They stood in the mist together for a long while then. Quiet.

Ray broke the silence.

"I almost couldn't go to my mother's funeral. Stood outside the church, little country-ass Georgia church, ducking the sun under a wood overhang. My cousin came and led me in by the hand, two minutes before the service. I was nineteen."

Julian didn't say anything, just angled his body closer, touched Ray on his arm, his shoulder.

Ray kept talking – about the musty smell of the pews, the minister's puffy jowls, the hymns. Kept talking all the way through to the burial, to the sound of the earth falling into the hole, thud-thud-thunder against the casket.

Ray's first words about it. Ten years after. The first time he'd ever talked about that day – a day so different, the Georgia sun so far from the New England fog.

★

The doorbell blast – shrill, electric – brings Ray back. To Brooklyn, to his studio, almost to now. Almost but not quite, so that the time between the buzz and Ezra walking up to his room is lost somewhere.

Until Ezra is right there, his feet mere inches from the apartment door, their actions choreographed by a force of matched heat.

Ezra drops his gym bag. "Yo, I'm crazy. . ."

"Sweaty." Ray finishes the sentence with him

Ezra's squinted eyes and cocked head say sorry, but Ray's grin signals sport, his stare levels a dare.

Ezra falls in step quick, a wink rearranges his expression. "Yo, I warned you."

"No doubt." Ray's eyes shift just long enough to slide down Ezra's torso and back up again.

Ezra still looks like a teenager – a soft mane frames his face, and an oversized T-shirt and baggy sweatpants hang off his lanky frame.

"So. . . shower?"

Ray shrugs in response. He takes a half-step closer to Ezra, reaches around him and grabs hold of his T-shirt. Runs two fingers of his right hand along the hem, lightly, from back around to the front. Flicks it loose, artful, to flash a brief strip of belly. Shrugs again.

"Oh yeah?"

"Yeah."

Still, Ezra takes his time raising the shirt to his shoulders, raising his arms to slip it past his head. Ray takes inventory of the flat stomach, the curls of hair loose, wild – a treasure trail. As Ezra's hands reach high above his head, the fabric swathed at his wrists, Ray springs. Quick, he reaches up, and grabs Ezra's wrists in place, his own fingers tightening into a warm cuff. Holding firm, he leans his face in close to the half-naked man, jamming his nose into the tight space where jawbone meets neck, he sniffs and traces a scented path to the hollow at Ezra's collarbone. Ray looks up to extend the dare – raise the ante – and Ezra's eyes are on him, piercing, expectant. Ray races his mouth to Ezra's lips, pries them apart.

And in the next moments – the now – Ray strides into the first buzz, fuelled by the musk scent. He angles his head to track the salt-sweat taste, getting tipsy. The call, "Sal...tee...", and response, "...Yea...ah", makes him high. Drunk, he lowers, shifts to reach a different pulse of muscle. More clothes are stripped and Ray's tongue reaches into damp hollows of intoxication. His fingertips stagger through coils of coarse hair.

Later, in the dark, Ray turns to see Ezra's leg slip back into sweatpants. Watches as he laces one sneaker, then the next. Goodbyes are simple, practical. A fist bump, "Gotta be out", a wink, "Later."

And later still, hours later, Ray finds his own sweats and sneakers. Jogs down the street to Fort Greene Park. He runs along the footpath, past the playground, up through the grove of coupled elms, down and around to find the steps. One hundred in all, leading up to the tower monument. Streaking through soft-edged spots cast by park lampposts, he takes the stairs two at a time. The first thirty-three and a landing, thirty-four and another landing, the final thirty-three, and the monument rises tall above its own lights. He turns and runs back down. Ten times – up and down – until he feels the ache in his legs. Until the sweat that he tastes is his own.

Then he stops. Ray sits at the top of the stairs staring out past the spilt pools of light, over the treetops and over Brooklyn's downtown roofs. It is too late for cruisers to be lurking, too early for the dog owners to be out socializing. This is a rare moment when New York feels like his alone. Manhattan lights – small, far – reflect the scene that he passed earlier on the bridge, the old stone, the new steel. The space.

On Saturday he sat in the kitchen while Julian cooked, watching him the way he used to watch his mother as a boy. On Sunday, Ray woke up in Julian's bed, his arm on the strong 'C' of Julian's curved back. He spent quiet, airy moments studying the ridges and lines of Julian's neck.

Yesterday, after he directed that tourist and his son to their train, he overheard the tow-headed kid ask a stream of questions. "Is this Brooklyn, Daddy? Are we gonna go meet Mommy? Is this the right way now, Daddy? How much farther? How long?"

Ray's mind fills with questions of his own. How far is it from where he sits to those buildings in Manhattan – as the crow flies? To that space? How far to Boston? To Georgia? How long does it take to get used to pockets of empty space. Can you fill them? Should you? Would it be too early to call Julian when he gets back to his studio? Would it be too late?

SECTIONS OF AN ORANGE

When police and store security responded to a 7:25 a.m.
alarm, they found a hole in a street display window at the
shop at 744 Fifth Ave., near 58th St.

The train bursts out of the subway tunnel onto elevated tracks
that climb up to the Smith Street Station. The gritty view –
stark contrasts of shadow and light, Brooklyn tenements
against Manhattan skyscrapers – launches me into the world,
reminds me that I haven't been out of my apartment in well
over a week. The days glided by with slick ease and I'm glad to
be doing something other than sitting in front of my computer, playing Free Cell and trying to break my last record in
Minesweeper.

The theft at the 63-year-old store was captured on
videotape, though the police said the footage was of poor
quality.

As I step off the F-train, I feel the rickety platform vibrate
under me, and a moment of uncertainty flashes through my
mind. I remember my encounter with Brian last month.
Truth be told, if he hadn't spotted me, I'd have walked right
past him. But he came walking towards me with body lan-

guage that seemed to say, from half a block away, that we'd planned to meet right there, he and I; and if not at that time, then five minutes earlier. On Fulton Street that day, he looked different – he'd cut his locks off, he'd gained a couple pounds, and aged a couple years – but he still looked good, especially when he smiled. When he smiled, he looked like a ten year old who'd just stoned down a juicy yellow mango and caught it before it hit the ground.

Getting past "Damn, it's been a long time" and "Oh man, I almost didn't recognize you," we'd talked outside South Portland Antiques, in a bright February light that masqueraded for spring. "Every last barber in Brooklyn jealous me," he explained as to why he wasn't working. "But that's a'ight 'cause I still have my photography, yuh know, my vision." I thought back to the last I'd heard about him, before this encounter: "Brian's off his rocker, yo," my regular barber had said. "I don't know if it's drugs, or what, but that cat was acting strange; they had to get rid of him." Not the response that my offhand question had been seeking, I'd discounted it at the time – "Nah, you're exaggerating again, Karly" – and then I'd changed the subject. I'd always had a thing for Brian and I hadn't been ready to give up on him so easily.

On Fulton that February afternoon, Brian was wearing a furry headband. He stooped down to tuck his jeans into black combat boots, talking all the while, bouncing through a stream of unconnected ideas – thoughts separate from the moment. But at intervals he returned to the sidewalk radiating charm.

"I can see that life's treating yuh well . . . yuh looking good."

I was flattered that he'd remembered me. "Yeah, it's good to see you man." At the end, he'd left with my phone number and a promise that I'd let him cut my hair.

A hit-and-run driver sparked mayhem on midtown Manhattan streets early yesterday – mowing down pedestrians in a wild, zigzag ride, police said.

Now before doubt turns me around, I walk the short blocks from the station to the address he'd given me. Brian answers the door.

"Yuh early," he says, in a black T-shirt, that looks too small, and grey sweatpants that look too big. "I thought we Trini people don' show up on time for nothing." I walk in as he pulls the door wide and steps back.

"First time for everything though," I say, glancing at my watch. "This place was easy to find." 'This place' is a small private house. He locks the front door saying that his sister and her husband are out at work. He's been staying here for a while – they let him use the basement.

I follow Brian down the hallway. Going down the stairs, our feet hit alternate steps, drumming an impromptu tribal rhythm. I sit down in a chair next to a battered dresser. Rough wood frames an abandoned space where a mirror once was, and bare spots show through cloudy lacquer like a telltale birth certificate. A large aluminium lamp, clamped to the top, cuts a sharp arc of light into the dim room, drawing a curve that a geometry class could convert to an equation in two variables.

Brian drapes a cloth around my shoulders, clipping it at the base of my neck.

"Damn, man, so when was the last time this head saw a pair of scissors?" he asks, laughing. His fingers wiggle through the long, tight curls of my hair, moving close to my scalp.

"Well it's not my fault man," I say laughing too. "I lost my barber – Karly, got married and moved down to Atlanta," I remind him.

"Hmm, huh," he mumbles. He reaches over to the dresser, opens a drawer that protests with a squeak of wood against wood, and pulls out a pair of scissors.

Standing behind me, he starts clip-snip, snip-clip passes in the air – a silver hummingbird flitting around my head. This is the start of the rite, and though I can't see him because there is no mirror, I know he's sizing up the hair – his canvas – snipping those blades together with practised flourishes. American barbers don't give me this sense of ceremony. No, this is a Trini-style thing that always takes me right back to my childhood. Here, with only the sound to create the image, it takes me back to my first haircuts in San Fernando. Gawd, I used to hate haircuts – I got in trouble with my father on many a Saturday over a trip to the barber. It started with Mr. Thorpe, an old friend of my dad's. They'd been in the same football club as teenagers, and played bridge together as adults. 'Torpers' did the clip-snip thing too, but back then it sounded menacing. Torpers had an extra digit on each hand – useless little joints next to each pinkie. One nub bounced in and out of focus under the scary blades on my right, and on the left, the other hung limp on the hand that held my squirming head in place.

As an adult, I'm still uneasy in the testosterone-laced world of the barbershop, uneasy with discussions of last night's game, and last week's conquest. As Brian's scissors go to work,

I find myself thinking, "I could get used to this special, private haircut arrangement."

> *The driver struck several people ending in Chelsea, where he plowed into a group of high-school students while zooming the wrong way down a side street. None of the injuries was life threatening.*

"Yo, I dig your mini soul-'fro, though," Brian says, early in the rite. And once he's renamed what I'd just been thinking of as my *unemployed-black-man-who-don't-care-look*, making it somehow legit, we agree on a trim – just shaping up the edges, making it a more definite statement. Snip-clip, clip-snip as cut hair falls quiet past my eyes. Before long there's a dark, irregular areola of hair sprinkled on the floor around me, and Brian's snip-clipping air again. In this final flourish, maybe only one or two strands of hair will be cut, maybe none – it's all about style and the perception of precision.

Next, the presentation of the mirror, normally matched with the slow spin of the barber chair to give a three-sixty view for inspection in the wall-mounted mirror. But today we have no swivelling barber chair and only a hand mirror, so I move it wide from left to right, angling my head and cutting my eyes to see the top and sides – settling for just a bit more than one hundred and eighty degrees. I nod my head once for the left angle, again for the top and finally a double nod on the right while saying my line, "Cool, cool." I pass the mirror back to him, he puts it down, undoes the clip at my nape and whips the cloth away from my body with a brisk matador's sweep.

Now, nearing the end of the ceremony, I stand so that he can brush off any wayward hair, my final movement in the *pas de deux*.

"Ah don' have a clothes brush, so don' mind this, okay," he says grinning. Once again we improvise: he grabs a little cloth and flicks it at my chest and shoulders, moving all around me, brushing my white T-shirt clean.

"Oh, gawd man," I say. "Yuh beatin' me like yuh is a obeah man trying to drive out a spirit." This time I have him laughing. Standing directly in front of me, he takes the joke to the next step, placing the palm of his right hand flat against my forehead, pushing my head back hard, and in the same movement his left arm comes around my back to steady me as I rock backwards.

"Be clean my son," he says in the priest's role. "Be cuh-lee-een." We're both laughing like kids now.

> *The driver scattered pedestrians like bowling pins. "He started hitting people and they kept falling and falling," said witness Gerald Cromwell, 31, of the Bronx.*

As we settle down, Brian says, "So, you want a drink – I think we need to offer a libation." Before I answer he's bouncing up the stairs, saying, "Lemme go and raid my brother-in-law's liquor stash."

I follow, trying to catch him. "Nah man, skip that." Not sure of what the living arrangement is here, I don't want to contribute to any domestic trouble. "You know what, I'm no big drinker anyway," I say, at the top of the stairs. It's brighter up here. "Let's just go to that bodega I passed on the way here. Get some beer, you know."

Brian agrees without too much discussion, he throws on a 'hoody', I grab my jacket, and soon we're walking down the street.

"Yuh know yuh ain' going to get no Carib in this 'hood," he says.

"Yeah, I know we not on Church Avenue, but I don't only drink Trini beer. . ."

He cuts me off with, "*Mira,* I hope you up for a Corona then."

"You wrong for that man, " I say. "Just wrong." And as if to prove my point, the corner store is stocked. "See, your ass was way off!" I say. "We got selection."

"True, true," he nods. "A'ight, you in charge, I drinks anything, so you can pick," he says wandering off. I reach for a six-pack of my favourite dark ale, but then I mix in a couple Heinekens to be safe.

I find Brian near the door. When he sees me coming over, he starts to juggle some oranges. He does a throw-catch thing with a couple of them and ends up dropping one back on the heap. The greying man behind the counter is looking at us evilly.

"Okay, I got the beer – something new for you to try," I say. "Let's roll."

"Ahm, okay if I get some of these oranges too?" Brian asks. I shrug agreement, surprised when he fills up a plastic bag with about ten of them.

At the counter, Brian grabs one of the oranges from the bag, tossing it high and then snatching it out of the air. The deli man jumps when Brian telegraphs a fake throw straight towards him. "Think fast," he says, catching it in his left hand as his right comes within a foot of the man's face. Brian laughs and the deli man's face registers fear, quickly followed by a braver annoyance. I pay and we walk outside. Feeling that I've just glimpsed the Brian of Karly's story, I remind myself that up to now he's been real cool. As we walk back up to his sister's house, though the sky is bright, I'm drawn to a striking new formation of metallic-gray clouds coming over the hill.

> *"I don't know what is happening in this city," said accountant Roselyn George, who suffered a broken ankle in yesterday's crash. "I got knocked down and one of my legs folded under me."*

Back in the basement, Brian puts on a cd, bragging that his boy brought it back from Carnival this year. "It's hot, you'll like it."

I open two bottles of Dos Equis, telling him, "You'll like this . . . it's cold." He groans at my bad joke, but grabs the beer that I hold out to him. Minutes later we're sitting on a futon mattress against the wall, drinking. He pulls out a pack of Bambu, a nickel bag from his pocket and starts rolling a joint. I'm thinking, "Damn, what the hell am I doing?" I've never hung out with this cat before, he didn't ask me if I smoke, or if I mind if he smokes, and I don't even know what the deal is with him. But I just sit back, secretly glad that he didn't ask. I haven't smoked weed in years, and right now I just feel like saying yes. If I'm not lying to myself, I know that I'm enjoying being here with him. I don't want to leave. Back when he'd started working at Nappy Image, I'd deliberately gone into the shop on a day when I knew Karly was off, just so I'd have an excuse to sit in Brian's chair. I'd wanted to be close while his grin lit up his face and his loud jokes brightened the whole shop.

By the time he's done rolling, the first two bottles are empty. He hands me the sleek joint, gets up to get two more bottles from near the dresser and adjusts the aluminium lamp so that it's now angled up, casting the light towards the ceiling. There's no more or less light in the room, but the glow is easier now, no longer a sharply defined area on the floor. He sits again, pulls a book of matches out of his pocket, strikes one and holds it out toward me. Again, no questions asked. I put the joint to my lips and puff until it's lit. Then I take a nice drag, and pass it over to Brian.

We sit in the long narrow room, beneath an artificial sky of smoke-clouds and aluminium sun, and the talk comes easy. A haze captures the low ceiling tiles, dancing around the exposed pipes and revelling in the upturned lamplight. I'm on a plane of calm that I haven't known in a long time; and I see that Brian's made the same journey too; and even more, I feel that we needed each other to get here. I pass the joint to him, warm from my lips on one end, glowing fire at the other. His fingers brush against mine. On his dark hands, the tendons and veins form a pattern like exposed roots. Energy transfers along an unseen path between us.

When I release the last herbal mist from my lungs, Brian takes a drag at what is now a roach, looking at me through tiny eyes.

"I want to take your picture," he says, unguarded in this found space. I don't react right away, the question bobbing up and down on the river of my thoughts. "With the oranges. When I saw the oranges I decided that I wanted to take your

picture with them." In the silence that follows, he exhales, puts
the roach out and looks back towards me, his eyes brushing my
neck, my jaw, and my mouth with a soft force, and then resting
deep inside my eyes.

"Where's the camera?" I reply.

After hitting George, the car lurched into the intersection
and swerved; barely slowing it turned left onto Seventh
Ave., mounting the curb and scattering commuters.

Soon, he comes balancing the oranges – piled on a shallow,
wooden bowl – in one hand, a professional-looking camera in
the other, and a plain white sheet folded over his arm. I remain
on the futon, watching the preparation: he drapes the sheet
over the seat of the chair, letting it fall in a pool on the floor;
he sets the bowl on the seat; he swings the light down to frame
the chair again; and then, he peels an orange, a knife orbiting
the golden fruit, disrobing it, and leaving bright strands of rich
natural fibre that fall on the chair and floor. Slicing the orange,
he looks over to me, for the first time since he's started
creating this scene. "Want some?" he asks, holding out half.

I take it and sit on the floor with my left arm resting on the
chair, bent at the elbow, I lean, my face close to the bowl, half
an orange in my right hand. I look up at Brian, about to ask him
"What now?" and he just picks the camera up and starts taking
pictures. I stare at him for a while, hearing the click of the
shutter, the advance of the film, watching him move. But I
have the munchies, and I bite into the orange, feeling the flesh
give against the pressure of my lips, mashing pulp against the
roof of my mouth. Each individual bead gives up its tiny

treasure, until sharp-sweet juice flows past my teeth. I slurp and eat – conscious on one level of the camera, yet enjoying being as messy as an unsupervised kid.

When the juice starts running down my chin and spilling unto my hands, I stop to push my shirtsleeves up over my elbows. But before I've picked the next half of the orange up, Brian is kneeling next to me. He rests the camera down on the floor, and his face is close to mine, staring. Holding the stare, he grabs the hem of my shirt, and pulls it over my head.

"I don' want yuh to dirty your clothes." Before I respond, he's standing again, camera back in hand. "A'ight, go ahead." Bare-chested now, I let the juice bead and run where it will, as Brian continues to snap.

Before long, I'm cutting the oranges in quarters and not just drinking the juice, but tearing pulp from pith, absorbed in the act. Brian comes over again. This time he grabs a section of orange, holds it six inches in front of my face, and steadying himself with one hand right next to me, he squeezes with the other hand. Juice falls through the air, hitting my chest, pooling at the centre and trickling down my belly. He waves his hand around, still squeezing, so that juice hits my face and shoulders, collecting in the hollow at my collarbone and forming a liquid necklace at my throat. His eyes follow the movement of his hand, a hand that seems to swallow the orange, tracing some deliberate pattern that only he knows. His fingers, smooth dark peninsulas that end in crowns of perfect pink nail, are wet now, and I want him to touch me. I want to bridge the scant inches between him and me, to follow the trail of his ring finger with my tongue until I reach the centre of his palm.

*After the crash, the man pulled his car over to the curb
and waited as a traffic cop walked toward him. But then
he sped away.*

But Brian doesn't touch me. Instead he grabs the camera and
starts shooting again. He's talking all the while now: "I had to
do this . . . since you first sat in the chair today . . . when I
reached in to cut your hair, you smelled like chocolate . . . and
I knew then, when I smelled the back of your neck, like
chocolate . . . like I was a pregnant woman, I had a craving,
man, a craving . . . I wanted some chocolate . . . then I saw the
oranges . . . I saw you covered in juice . . . I had to see you . . . and
drink man . . . just drink . . . smell you, chocolate and orange . . .
tell me it don' feel good, eh . . . cause damn, it looks so good
. . . you have lil shiny beads of juice on your neck . . . nice, nice
. . . like plenty, plenty little diamonds, man . . . on your
beautiful skin . . . and that juice baby, yeah . . . so good."

*At 18th St., the driver turned right as Pablo Vargas
walked to work at a nearby bistro. Vargas jumped back
but couldn't get out of the way as the car again bounced
onto the curb. "I thought the guy had a heart attack and
lost control," said Vargas, 36.*

Then the camera's down for the third time. Now when he
nears me, he doesn't stop all those inches away. His lips are
soft on my neck and his fingers trace thick lines of electric
current over my arms and chest.

Then, his mouth sticky and hot right next to my ear, he
says, "I want you to be naked, man . . . naked." And when I close

my eyes, and sigh deep, he knows that the answer is yes. While
he loads new film into the camera, I drape the sheet in a wide,
loose sash over my shoulder and between my legs. I feel cool
cotton cloth gather around me, and he matches my thoughts,
telling me how good the white looks next to my skin. He snaps
slower now and we take our time, changing positions, explor-
ing poses: sitting on the chair with the sheet on my lap,
holding the bowl in outstretched arms; standing with the
white cloth shirred at my waist, knotted in front and falling to
my knees; the sheet wrapped around my back, crossed at my
collar and knotted at my nape, the bowl resting between my
wide spread legs. I remember playing "fashion show" with my
cousin Gail when we were young, excited but afraid that I'd
get caught "acting like a little girl". But when the fabric is
girding my middle and slung over my shoulder, Brian tells me
that I look like an African prince. I feel like a man, like all that
is a man, aware of each taut, strong curve of muscle that I wear
– raw and real – with the orange's sugar and my salt about me.
I'm strong through the lens of his wanting, male through his
eyes. Chocolate and orange, muscle and cotton, a camera's
lens and Brian's vision, fit together like sections of an orange,
making me feel whole and natural now.

★

Later, I walk to the train station with a newfound posture that
lifts my step and props me as I surf the urban waves of the
subway. I fight an uneasiness that's vague and wispy in the grey
moments before sleep, but becomes so specific, as I rise, that
I can almost smell it. Brian calls later that day. "Just wanted to

let you know I had a great time yesterday Chocolate Man. . . Can't wait to see you again. . . I have a great idea for us. . . Just wait, gonna make you shine, baby." I don't know Brian well enough to plot his next step and I wonder if I'll spend the next days and weeks avoiding strange calls or enjoying the vision of an eccentric artist. I'm worried, but thinking all the while of accessories for our next encounter – silk and mangoes, raffia and honey, body paint and flowers.

Days later, in this web of afterglow and anxiety and desire, I'm stopped in my tracks as I walk past a newsstand. Brian's face, black and white, beneath a tabloid headline: **SWIPE-AND-RUN RAMPAGE.**

> *After a jewelry heist yesterday, the thief sparked mayhem on Manhattan streets, plowing a stolen car into crowds in a ride of terror. Almost $200,000 worth of jewelry was stolen from the Van Cleef & Arpels store on Fifth Avenue early yesterday after someone smashed a small front window, grabbed the jewelry and fled, the police said. "No one made any penetration into the store," said a spokeswoman for the jewelry store. She declined to say what was stolen, but police identified the items as a $98,000 necklace, a $72,000 bracelet and a $25,000 ring. The theft at the toney jeweler was captured on videotape, and the items were found later in the green Buick Regal driven by a hit-and-run driver who was cornered by cops in Chelsea.*

RING GAMES

In a fine castle, do you hear my Cissy-o?
In a fine castle, do you hear my Cissy-o?

Brian walks into the jewelry store on Fifth Avenue and the sales staff look up. It is minutes past five-thirty and the store will close soon. Brian does not know that this is Van Cleef and Arpels. If he did know the name, it would mean nothing to him. But the store is small, quiet and elegant. As the door closes behind him, the familiar New York street – the bus exhaust, the hotdog carts and rushing pedestrians, the honking taxis – is replaced by this other space: clear gentle light, graceful easy curves, and low classical music. There is no lobby, no anteroom. Once past the door, Brian stands on soft green carpet, surrounded by matching upholstered armchairs scattered around the room. His first impression is that he's walked into a stranger's private drawing room.

He makes a mental adjustment. Brian, ready to lower his voice in pitch and volume. Brian, ready to tilt his chin just so. Brian, ready to flash his smile. Brian, ready to charm.

The middle-aged salesman nearest the door turns his pin-striped frame, focused anew on straightening an already straight stack of paperwork. At a desk on the right, the saleswoman in the high-necked cream silk dress lowers her blonde bun back to the grey-haired woman seated before her. A catwalk-thin girl stands easy in the rear. She wears a white blouse with a ruffled collar. She alone continues to look at Brian as he walks over to one of the display cases. Her eyes sweep from toe to crown. Brian, in the uniform of the streets: Timberlands, baggy blue jeans, bulky sweatshirt. She has a hard time assessing him, pegging him into the correctly shaped hole. Rich man, Poor man, Beggarman, Thief? Rapper? Messenger? Homeless man? Thug?

Brian has been walking around the city all afternoon on a mission. A mission made more difficult because he was unsure of what exactly he sought. For a while he'd looked for a location, some magic place. Crystal light flooded his subway car, winking as the Q-train rode past the crisscross beams of the Manhattan Bridge. And Brian thought, "Maybe." Patience and Fortitude guarded shallow concrete stairs in the shadow of the Public Library. "Here?" he wondered. Neon billboards stood in iridescent cubist planes over Times Square. "Perhaps." The grail, veiled in shadow, but the purpose clear. To be with Chocolate Man again, to impress him, recapture the special moments.

> *Ours is the prettiest. Do you hear my Cissy-o?*
> *Ours is the prettiest. Do you hear my Cissy-o?*

In Van Cleef and Arpels, minutes before closing, Brian looks down at a case filled with jewelry and believes that he's found it. "Yes." Chunky luminous pearls, strung into bracelets and necklaces, cascade over putty-coloured velvet platforms in a case whose only other occupants are diamonds and pearls clustered together into starry earrings. Brian stands looking. Separate from any conscious adjustment, his head does tilt and his lips do part in a smile. His mind whirls, contemplating which film speeds and apertures would best capture the lustre of the gems.

"Good afternoon." The thin girl is standing nearer to Brian now. Though her eyes have not left him, she is as yet undecided about how to peg him.

"Yes. . . hello." Brian looks up at the face framed by frills, and his own expression is open and clear. "These are nice, really."

"Thank you."

Brian shifts his gaze to another case. The displays are arranged in cubes of glass, like delicate museum artifacts. In this next one, bright stones glimmer midst a maze of miniature twigs. Topaz, amethysts, and sapphires vie with emeralds for his attention.

"Nice," he says again. "Tell me about these."

"Certainly," the thin girl starts her explanation – the quick version. "These pieces feature the finest gemstones from Asia and Africa. . . fine because of the colour and clarity of the stones. . .all hand-mounted especially for Van Cleef and Arpels."

"Wait, I'm sorry." Brian stops her. "Before you go on, I should. . ." and in the moment when she looks up, he smiles and almost whispers, ". . . I'm Brian Gadson."

"Mr. Gadson," she says reaching out a pale hand. "I'm Kit."

"Brian, please."

And the thin girl, Kit, can feel the eyes of the blonde bun and the pin-striped suit watching her. But Brian holds her gaze, guiding her eyes back to the case. Kit, still deciding. She has more than one reason for wanting him to be legitimate. She is the new associate, the unproven. She's seen her colleagues sum up and dismiss certain people as they walk in the door – "Lookie-Lou. . . Tourist. . . Pretender" – and she hates it. Kit's known men who look like Brian, she's danced with them at Nell's – barely clothed and sweating, and sometimes she's been with them later – sweating more, unclothed.

"So, did you have something special in mind?" Kit asks.

Yes. Brian does have something special in mind. Brian the photographer, inspired, as artists have been inspired through the ages. Brian the man, moved, as suitors are in classic tales of love. Brian the lured, enticed by the gems, the settings, the feel of this room. Pictures of Chocolate man, photographic images, sharpen in his mind's dark room.

"Special? For sure."

He is fairly beaming now. He has the object of his quest within reach. And he has an ally in the chase. After years of observing people's behaviour, observing as an outsider, Brian recognizes the rare moment when he's won an ally.

> *We want one of them. Do you hear my Cissy-o?*
> *We want one of them. Do you hear my Cissy-o?*

Brian, the outsider. In his first year of primary school, he'd been the tallest boy in the class and the teacher had assigned him to a desk at the rear wall, and placed him at the end of every formation for assembly, for class outings. He was big enough to be a good back for the football team, but could never manage to stop the ball as it spun past him on the field. He was quiet and appeared bookish, but was never smart enough to be one of the "bright boys".

During his eleventh year, he came close to carving an identity for himself. At recess one day, Andres bumped into him and caused him to lose control of the *Flavour-ice* that he was eating. His frozen red treat bumped against his white shirt, skid down his khaki shorts and crashed – flaring ruby – to the dusty schoolyard. Brian reacted to the picture that flashed through his head: his mother's face as she saw his stained uniform. He grabbed Andres at the collar and spun him, slamming him back first, into a wall. As a circle formed around them, Andres tried to hand Brian money to buy a new ice. Brian knocked the coins away. The result was that the school *badjohns* didn't respect him because he threw away money (something they'd never do) and his other classmates stayed even further from him than before, out of fear. He continued his childhood looking in.

Now Brian and Kit are looking through spotless glass together.

"If you like diamonds, you should see this collection." They walk to another display case.

"Oh yeah. . . you know your stuff, Kit."

Encouraged by Brian's ease, Kit is ready to rule out Poor man. "This cuff. . . white gold. . . set with pavé diamonds, almost fifteen karats in weight."

Brian notices for the first time that each display case is labelled with small black letters. Here: COMET'S TAIL PAVÉ DIAMOND BRACELET 14.75kt TOTAL WEIGHT. The script is spare and simple – sleek. Discreet. It also says: $85,000.

"Of course, we carry a number of different earrings that would be delightful with this."

"Of course." Brian looks at Kit and smiles, surprised by the cool delivery that belies his sticker shock.

Two pairs of earrings dangle at different heights from knotty, natural twigs. A diamond choker swirls casually over vibrant green leaves.

> *Which one do you want? Do you hear my Cissy-o?*
> *Which one do you want? Do you hear my Cissy-o?*

Brian steels himself for a host of questions from Kit: Is this for a special occasion? A surprise? Who's the lucky lady? Do you have a particular preference? Special stones? A set price range?

Instead Kit says, "Please have a look around. Enjoy."

She steps back a few paces – quietly – standing pleasantly, near the back of the store. This is policy. There is no hard sales pitch at Van Cleef and Arpels. So, alone again, Brian stands entranced by the beauty of the stones.

He is comfortable here, more comfortable than he's been all day on the streets of Manhattan, more comfortable than he has been over the past weeks living in his sister's house, more than he had been cutting hair at Nappy Images, before he was asked to leave. Here, surrounded by beauty and elegance, he's occupied with ideas and memory. Yesterday, the impromptu photoshoot. That was good. And comfortable. Chocolate Man. The rich cocoa smell, the tight smooth skin. So good, so comfortable inside. Tomorrow must bring more. Must. Chocolate Man again, inside again. Tomorrows and yester-days crisscross like ribbons on a maypole.

★

It's two o'clock at the Claxton Bay EC School. It's dry season in Trinidad. The afternoon air is stagnant and hot, and Miss Primus has brought her Standard Two class outside to play games.

"Is not just a break for me, it just makes no sense to try to force people' children to do school work inside a classroom hot-hot like a coal-pot oven."

She and her class – five little girls in pinafores and six skinny boys in khaki shorts – are gathered under the shade of a plum tree. Brian and the other six-and-seven-year-olds are ordered in a circle – boy, girl, boy, girl – holding hands and singing.

> *"Farmer in the dell, farmer in the dell,*
> *hi-ho, the dairy-o, the farmer in the dell."*

Brian doesn't know what a dell is, but he's glad to be outdoors – away from afternoon spelling lessons. A bold breeze blows up from the sea, through the mangrove, past the fish stands and over the Main Road. This one, this bold breeze, is strong enough to climb even farther: up the hill, through the gravestones in the churchyard and all the way to the plum tree. It brushes under his chin, dips under his blue shirt and whisks away a film of sweat. This breeze tickles his ear.

Brian is not the Farmer, but he doesn't mind.

Ian is the Farmer and as he parades happy along the outside of the circle, Miss Primus calls out the next verse. "The farmer takes his wife." The children in the circle keep singing, "...takes his wife... the farmer takes..." as Ian exercises his power to choose the best 'wife'. Ian picks Shirley and there are cheers and giggles. Then Ian and Shirley skip around the ring together. The game continues, they sing on, swinging hands and cheering at each selection. Wife, nurse, son, daughter, maid – Miss Primus adds just enough characters to the song to fit her class of eleven. "The nurse takes the maid, the nurse takes the maid."

Brian isn't any of these. Not the farmer, not the son, not the friend. He stares far out to the gulf, where an oil tanker sails toward the refinery at Point-a-Pierre.

"The cheese stands alone. The cheese stands alone."

★

A metal jangle brings Brian back to Van Cleef and Arpels as the Pin-striped Associate toys with a set of keys. Pinstripe walks over to Kit and speaks in hushed tones that are no louder than the sound of his footfall on carpet. "Time" . . . whisper, murmur, ". . . your client," . . . whisper.

"Mr. Gadson. . ." Kit seems tense.

"*Mister* Gadson?" Brian's eyebrows arch.

"Brian." She smiles.

"Kit."

"I'm terribly sorry, I feel so bad rushing you, but we, Van Cleef and Arpels, close at six o'clock."

"Uh huh."

"I don't know that I've provided the level. . ."

"Kit, we're cool. . . yeah, cool."

"Here's my card. Please accept my personal invitation to return so that we can be of more service."

"Your card."

"And again, my apologies, Brian."

"Thanks Kit. . . yeah thanks."

What will you give him? Do you hear my Cissy-o?
What will you give him? Do you hear my Cissy-o?

Brian is back on Fifth Avenue. As quickly as it had begun minutes earlier, Brian's time inside Van Cleef and Arpel's is over. Brian outside – amidst Fifth Avenue's tourists and fashion plates, commuters and cabs – outside.

He turns right on Fifty-Seventh Street, walking west in the sun's waning path. Thinking only that he has to feel again what he felt yesterday with Chocolate Man. Believing that he has found the key to guarantee that it will happen. But how will he convert this discovery into a reality?

He walks through the crowded streets of Manhattan, crablike – one block west, two blocks south. He passes glass panes, cloth awnings and concrete slabs – offices, stores and restaurants. Hunks of metal roll past the periphery of his view. Cars and buses are no more real to him now than price tags. Quick beings dart in and out of his sightlines. A redhead in an aqua shawl brushes past his left shoulder. A poodle, tethered to a man with a salt-and-pepper beard, sniffs a hydrant. Nothing breaks through to his consciousness. Night is falling – a natural orange light is fading, being replaced by the City's sparkling lights.

His thoughts swirl, looping between yesterday afternoon's surprise, today's find, and a picture of tomorrow that hangs like a neon star before him.

Yesterday began simply with a haircut, and then transformed under the scent of cocoa butter and clouds of ganja smoke. The vision had come to him, as he'd cut Chocolate Man's hair in his sister's basement. And afterwards, after the haircut, after a joint – it had become real. "I want to take your picture," he'd said, in an unguarded moment. "Since you first sat in the chair today. . . when I reached in to cut your hair, you smelled like chocolate . . . and I knew then, when I smelled the back of your neck. . ." Chocolate Man had replied, "Where's the camera?" Magic photographs: beads of light, dark flesh stretched taut over ropes of muscle, currents of promise made visible.

Yes, it had been magic. Magic that turned fragrance into a clear, vibrant image. Magic that turned an old client from the barbershop into a muse, a partner. Magic that turned a barber into a photographer, an outsider into a hero. Magic that made passion pure, that made sex more than a game of control. Yesterday a magic connection. Today, a doorway to tomorrow's promise.

★

"Yo, lemme get a Snickers and a Sunkist," Brian says, waiting at a newsstand on 8th and 51st.

The intervening streets have made no impression on him, other than to heighten his craving.

"Yo."

In the kiosk, a young Indian man stands on a raised platform. He reaches forward to hand a pack of cigarettes to a blue-haired woman. He makes change, and then hands her a pack of matches too.

"A Snickers and a Sunkist."

A chubby white man, Brian's age, wearing a denim shirt, reaches past him for a pack of Juicyfruit gum. The vendor holds out a hand for the quarter, his fingertips stained by years of coins and bills. Then he turns to wait on a girl with long black hair, who has just walked up.

"Yes, miss."

"I'm after him," the brunette says, motioning to Brian. She looks a bit like Kit.

"Snickers. . . a Sunkist."

"Oh, I didn't. . ."

"Yeah, you ain' hear me? Right. You ain' see me. . ."

The vendor places a can on the counter, and then gestures toward the shelf for Brian to get the candy bar himself. The frayed cuff of a white shirt pokes from below the sleeve of a battered, unmatched suit jacket – dingy white against cheap grey stripes. Brian grabs the candy and soda, flings down a bill, some coins.

". . .Asshole!"

Manhattan. Brian notices, now, the people who share the sidewalks with him. These people – their lives, their worlds, their thoughts. He feels them all watching him, assessing him – no look indifferent. Brian is never simply 'man on the street' to any of them. Some give him a wide birth and pretend to ignore him, like Indian Vendor, like Pinstripe. Others cross his path, cut him off, no acknowledgement. And maybe even worse, the ones – women and men – who size him up: from solid thighs to smooth full lips, some stop at broad shoulders or even at crotch. Brian on the avenue: beggarman; thief; morsel of cheese, alone.

He notes each look on this street. Each one matches a look he's seen before. From childhood in Claxton Bay: teachers grading him, classmates on the playground. From years later: a sideways look from his brother-in-law as he reached into the refrigerator for milk, or dialled a phone number; hungry looks from customers in the barbershop, customers who hit on him, picked him up. After he'd come to The States, he'd developed, become something sexually desirable. But. . . always with those people, Brian was either worker or toy. Service on demand. Brian, finally picked, finally – years and years after Claxton Bay EC School, after The Farmer, The Nurse, The Dog – picked, yet still alone.

But yesterday. . . yesterday brought something new, something special. Chocolate Man made him feel different. Brian picked. Brian created scene. Brian set the pace. . . Chocolate Man kept up, matched every step, joined him. In new spaces: art and liberation.

In a fine castle...do you hear my Cissy-o?

After the farmer in the dell, Miss Primus's class played 'Brown Girl/Brown Boy in the Ring' and 'Jump Around'. Then they played 'In a Fine Castle', a ring game full of adventure and possibility. The boys formed one circle and the girls another. As they swung hands, they sang, calling back and forth to each other – first the boys, then the girls. Boys, girls, boys. And as the song progressed, a silent agreement developed. Each line was repeated to form a verse, and each verse brought a suitor closer and closer to securing the hand of the fair one.

> *In a fine castle, do you hear my Cissy-o?*
> *Ours is the prettiest, do you hear my Cissy-o?*
> *I want one of them. Do you hear my Cissy-o?*
> *Which one do you want? Do you hear my Cissy-o?*
> *I want Chocolate Man! Do you hear my Cissy-o?*
> *What will you give him? Do you hear my Cissy-o?*
> *I'm gonna give him an orange, do you hear my Cissy-o?*
> *That don' suit him, do you hear my Cissy-o?*
> *I'm gonna give him a diamond ring! Do you hear my Cissy-o?*
> *Then you can have him!*

Van Cleef and Arpels: small square-cut store window. . . glowing, within. . . bright like the tip of a joint. Face inches from glass. . . fingertips brush pane. Flavour-ice cool, Brian stands, stares. . . long moments. . . gems, inside. "Finest gemstones from Asia and Africa." He must not go empty handed to Chocolate Man. . . not home. . . to sister's dark basement.

Payphone. . . He drops a quarter. . . dials number, memorized like Cissy-o beat. Answering machine. "Wanted to let you know I had a great time yesterday, Chocolate Man. . . Can't wait to see you again. . . Got a great idea for us. . . Just wait. . . Gonna make you shine baby."

Central Park South. Brian on wooden bench. Brian looking ahead. Before him: luxe, stone facades. . . skyward. . . hotel suites. . . penthouse apartments. Manhattan lives and thoughts have penetrated into his world. . . broken past remembered farmers. . . through closed circles. . . bringing golden hopes, shimmering mirages. He doesn't see green trees behind: leaves, limbs and bark break through cold dirt, waiting patient for tomorrow's sun. Wind, granite edged. . . Brian pulls the sweatshirt hood over his head, leans back. . . Electric lights mask distant true stars.

MR. PARKER'S BEHAVIOUR

. . .cheaper to pay for a bicycle pump than to see the end of the world.
– Earl Lovelace, "The Bicycle Pump"

At noon when Agatha is finished laying the table, she knocks on Mr. Parker's study door and calls him for lunch, as usual. She walks back to the kitchen for the jug of grapefruit juice in the fridge and returns to find him sitting down, bold-as-brass, in nothing but his drawers and slippers – half-naked at the dining room table.

Agatha Stewart has been working for the Parker family for her entire adult life, plus a few more years to boot. Her mother had been the (senior) Parker's housekeeper, and when she herself was old enough she'd helped with the elaborate preparations for Christmas and Easter in the Parker home. Cuthbert, the youngest Parker boy, got married to a prissy little bookworm, just when Agatha was ready to finish school, and Agatha's first official job was cooking and cleaning for them. This is the only full-time job she has ever known. So when Cuthbert Parker shows up for Sunday lunch wearing nothing but his skivvies, she has every right to be shocked. And angry. In all the donkey years with this man, she has never seen him behave so lowdown and base. Just what exactly could have gotten into his head? He really expected her to sit at the table with him like that?

Agatha stands under the carved woodwork of the doorway between the kitchen and the dining room, with the jug suspended in her hand. She stares at the table, its two places perfectly set, the correct parts of a good Sunday meal – stewed pork, callaloo, macaroni pie, salad – ready in the centre, serviettes folded, glasses gleaming, and Cuthbert Parker seated in his usual position. Finally, she puts the jug in its place, a stormy tide of juice breaking near the rim. She spins around on her heels and makes a silent retreat into her bedroom.

Agatha sits at the edge of her bed and it feels like a precipice. In truth, she doesn't know if she should be more angry about his rudeness or because he spoiled their Sunday lunch. Since his wife died six years ago, Agatha and Mr. Parker have sat down once a week to eat together. The rest of the week she eats in the kitchen, after she's served him. But one day a week, they sit down like two grown people and have a nice meal together. So, exactly what could possess him to spoil it today? She pulls out her bible to read her favourite psalm and ends up reading the whole book of Psalms. Agatha doesn't go back out to clean up the table until it's dark.

The next day Agatha tries to go back to normal. For the whole day, she just doesn't let that vulgarity come back into her head. But as the week goes on, she starts to notice something else. It's a small something compared to the outrageous Sunday business, but Agatha knows Mr. Parker inside and out. She knows his best traits and his worst habits. Agatha knows that Mr. Parker is a man who wakes up at a quarter to six every morning that God gives him health and strength –

even since he retired from being principal. She knows that she has to sweep under his bed carefully, because Mr. Parker never learned how to pick up his fingernail and toenail clippings.

Anyway, the thing is that Mr. Parker starts eating funny. Tuesday morning, Agatha serves him breakfast as usual – hot green tea, two slices of buttered bread, and one soft-boiled egg in the ceramic eggcup. She sees him drinking from the saucer when she walks by the table, but that is just another of his bad habits: he never waits for the tea to cool off, he pours it in into the saucer in batches and sips. No, the funny thing is that when Agatha clears off the table, the teacup is still full, and the milk pitcher is empty.

The same thing happens again on Wednesday morning. On top of that, when Agatha goes to wash the wares, the crusts from his bread are still on the plate. If that is not enough, the sunny yolk is staring up at her from the bottom of the eggcup. She stands by the sink for a good minute with that plate in one hand, and the eggcup in the other – looking from one to the next. Mr. Parker was never a big eater, but he never leaves any food back on his plate either. Agatha finally walks over to the rubbish bin and throws the brown crusts away. Washing the yolk down the drain, she hears Mr. Parker's voice in her head, saying "Waste not want not." How many times had she heard him say that to his wife over the years?

By Thursday, that business with the breakfast is still going on, so Agatha decides to make Mr. Parker's favourite, okra-and-rice, for lunch. When she makes a point to walk past the table while he's eating, she sees him pushing aside all the okra and only eating the rice. Now she is just plain confused. All of a sudden, at the end of every meal, there is food left back on his plate, the brown crusts, the green okra, all the meat and even the tomatoes, (but not the cucumber). This man, who she knows inside and out, is only eating white food!

Just what is going on with Mr. Parker?

Agatha lies down that night, in a state of confusion, interrupted at intervals by spasms of worry. Something is definitely wrong. She has been working for this man since – before he was a man. Now, something is happening to him. For the first time since she was a young woman, Agatha starts wondering about her life. Has she made the wrong choices? Is she going to be punished for some ill deeds?

For her whole life Agatha Stewart has just done the things that made sense to her. There was never any big set of planning and worrying about 'if' and 'what' and 'why'. She just did. When she was fourteen, her mother said "Come to the Parker house and help me polish all that set of teakwood them people want shine-up for the holiday." Agatha said, "Yes, Mamma." A few years later, when Cuthbert Parker's mother asked her if she wanted to go and work for her son and her new daughter-in-law, Agatha said, "Yes, Miz P." So what if she never had any husband, never had any children? She always had a roof over her head, food in her belly and a new dress to wear to church on Christmas. Besides the work was easy. That dainty little social woman that Cuthbert married not only never learned how to run a house, but never managed to give the man any children either. So the house was never overrun with dirty nappies, little girls' jacks or little boys' marbles.

All these thoughts are running wild through Agatha's head

while she's in her bedroom. In truth, she can't even settle enough to read one bible verse properly. She gets up, turns off the light and lies down in the bed with the moonlight coming through the window. Seems like she didn't even have sense enough to close the curtain properly tonight. What it is going on with this man? Is contagious, too?

And the fact of the matter is, the whole night goes by just like that, with Agatha lying down in the moonlight. A lifetime of questions and a jumble of emotions flood her mind. She starts to nod off a little bit, but a *jumbie bird* in the sapodilla tree starts a blasted "hoot, hoot" calling, and she wakes up with her confusion becoming sadness. Maybe she shouldn't ever have sat down to eat with Mr. Parker. Maybe this is a punishment. Maybe she shouldn't be letting him come into her bedroom on Sunday nights.

Just before daybreak, her eyelids start getting heavy. But before she can even catch forty winks, the damned mongrel dog next-door starts barking like a wild animal. Again is worry she worrying when the sun is coming up. What is to become of her in her old age? Is not bad enough that she never had a husband and a family, but the little comfort that she knows must slip away too? Finally, a cock starts crowing and she gives up on sleep. She walks over to open the window for some fresh air and Cuthbert Parker is outside watering plants naked as the day he was born.

"Lord, put a hand!"

Sure now that no peace lies in her bedroom, Agatha escapes to the kitchen. Maybe comfort could be found in her daily work, solace in the room that is her domain, solely. She scrubs the floor, the old fashioned way, on her knees. The hard-bristled brush suds and raises a regular percussive song that almost, just almost, drowns out thought of Cuthbert Parker and questions of tomorrow. Later, after she's hand-dried the floor, after she's banished any speck of dirt to distant corners, Agatha begins Mr. Parker's breakfast. But with Mr. Parker's daily egg inches just inches from the boiling water, she pauses. Agatha retrieves a box of Quakers Oats from the back of the cupboard. She slowly boils the cereal to baby-food softness, sweetens it with condensed milk, and pours the creamed, steaming porridge into a tall white mug.

Mr. Parker is seated at table at his appointed time, as Agatha serves the oatmeal. He is dressed – fully and properly dressed. "Yes, nothing too hard about changing to porridge instead of toast and eggs," she thinks. And when she cleans up after breakfast, there are no disturbing egg yolks or crusts of bread to discard. As Agatha washes the morning dishes, she plans this Sunday's lunch. Baked chicken served without the skin, a nice white gravy, and some potato salad, or the macaroni pie baked with a foil lid to stay, well white, yes white. Yes, and as Agatha and Mr. Parker sit, she will remind him about his longtime plan to build a wall around the yard.

"Yes, get the man to come and start laying down the bricks this week coming," she'll say. "Keep out alla them Reed Street dogs and fowls, get some privacy."

ONE, TWO, THREE – PUSH

Push walks past a rusting iron gate into the gallery opening. Red Hook building, tough to find. Close to the river, neighbourhood unfamiliar. The room's buzzing. Push spies the promised open bar close to the door and heads over.

– You a painter? light-skinned sister with braids asks him.

– No. Push doesn't break stride.

The bar's a self-service deal: battered door straddling sawhorses. Glasses of red and white in rows. Red going faster. Ice-filled tub on the floor. Push grabs a beer, takes a long swig and stands-by, checking out the room. *Radicals Re-Envisioned*. It's a joint showing, six different artists, mixed media, paintings and sculpture, video bouncing grainy against a far wall. Mixed crowd. Push isn't here for the crowd. He's only here to see his boy Dave's stuff.

Green metal mass rises high in the centre of the room – mutant cactus. Dave standing nearby. Talking to the chick with the braids. Another woman Push recognizes as Dave's agent. A small group in denim-blues and nightclub-blacks. Dave gestures toward the cactus, the group turn and look. Except the chick with the braids. Staring at Push, still.

Shit, here we go again, Push thinks. He tilts the bottle to his head and lowers it, watches the liquid slosh 'round the halfway mark. Narrow sargasso sea.

Dismiss that "painter" question, Push. Chalk it up to his clothes.

College friends used to say that he had a sense of occasion. Push dressed New England preppie at a Saturday football game. Safety-pin-spotted punker at a dive bar later same night. Tonight, this linen shirt, black and billowing big, ridged with embroidery. Unworn before, but right tonight with blue jeans chopped-off at the calf and Chuck T's splattered red-blue-yellow from last Carnival's *Jouvert* band. Yeah, easy to get lost in a Carnival band. So yeah, maybe tonight he does just look like a painter.

Push finishes the beer and Dave's still surrounded. Grabs another. Starts walking around, surveys. Through clumps of people, past paintings that don't hold his eye, ends up at a corner installation. A huge painting leans against the wall, seven or eight feet tall. Oil or acrylic. Laid thick on canvas. On the floor before it, a scattering of objects. Push stands, taking inventory: flask of clear liquid, yellow and green label, overproof rum; drum, roughraw wood, hairy goatskin cover – *rumdrum*, *rumdrum* – candles, burning and dripping white; a cocoyea broom, palm-frond ribs dried and bound with a swatch of red cloth.

– It takes you there doesn't it? The question comes cozy. Interrupts. Just as the red from the broom was drawing him into the image. Into the woman's red sash.

He looks up. Expects to recognize the questioner. Instead, an Asian man with dreadlocks pulled into a ponytail, blond tips sticking out.

– Huh?

– Takes you there. . . Powerful, man. . . You were like. . . far away.

– Uh-huh.

– That woman, intense. . . like there's this real raw energy inside her. . . like radiating, right?

– Yeah.

Both, looking. Frame dominated by a thin, dark-skinned woman. *Granny would call her hard-and-dry.* Her head's wrapped in maljo blue cloth: intense, primary colour knotted at the forehead. Her cheekbones jut smooth parentheses around her eyes and nose. Her figure, all limbs, drawn in angles and lines. The red sash at her waist barely holds the white frills of her skirt onto her body in near flight.

– Wonder what that feels like?

Guy seems okay. Someone to kill time with until Dave's available.

– She looks free, he says. Mother Earth, free.

– Yeah? *Free radicals, organic chemistry, junior year science requirement.* Push tries to remember the prof's name. *Majors, Magi?*

To Push, the woman just looks like Tanté Tilda, his grandmother's near sister. Tilda, they say, picked up four children and left a druken husband, started over.

– Man, I was looking at you from across the room, the Asian man speaks with the cadence of a bad beatnik poet. Knew I'd want to hear what you thought of this one.

– Yeah? *This one? Or you? Yeah, yeah.*

– Yes. By the way, my name's Kûkai; it's great to meet you.

– Cheers. Push raises his beer bottle. I'm. . .

– Yes, I saw your show last fall. Great stuff. I really felt your passion.

Great, Dude thinks he knows who I am. Push toys with the idea of playing along, embodying an icon for Kûkai. But. Hasn't got it in him to play these days.

It's the beard, though, the beard and the hair. During his teens Push cultivated a shadowy moustache, feeling more mature the thicker it grew in. In his twenties, he sported the Malcolm X look, along with Spike, Denzel and a Million Men marching to DC. Once he hit thirty, longslim sideburns – blunt geometric strips to square off his jaw. Round peg, square jaw. And a clean upper lip, always a clean upper lip to hook compliments on his kissable mouth. But always shaved cheeks and jaw, shaved neck. Always, save the past months. God save the queen.

Now Push wears a full beard. Not so much wears it, as he'd sported the goatees and sideburns – he never decided to "wear" it. No, the beard developed, kinda scraggly at first, growing longer and thicker in time. Buffer of beard. Dark one-way lens to let in select rays of light, like Dave, block the rest. No compliments please.

But with the beard had come misconceptions.

– I didn't get a chance to talk to you at your show. . . Kûkai starts.

– My show?

– . . .but I knew I'd get a chance to vibe with you sometime. Believe that.

– Nah, somebody else, Push almost begs Kûkai to see his mistake.

– You. Yes you, last. . .

Push feels Kûkai's eyes on his back as he walks away. Maybe he can get Dave alone now. At least he'll find the painting, check out his boy's shit, right? Thing is, he wasn't ready to leave that last installation. It did kinda take him away. Kûkai

got that right, even if he ID'd Push wrong. That woman, like
Tanté Tilda, bursting vibrant from a background of shadow
figures and deep forest night. If he'd watched for a just a little
longer, intent, he'd hear the drum pulsing a Shango beat, hear
the forest moaning, hear the woman cry out loud. He would
hear her scream. Her scream, a cry from his own core, from
beneath his layers of painted quiet.

Push never got to scream when his last relationship fizzled.
Not allowed to scream for one that short, right? Still the three-
month-waste-of-time left him weary, wary. Warlike. It doesn't
really matter how much you try.

And didn't he swallow the scream, unuttered, when he sat
in his boss's office for his last performance review, the review
that matched the prior one almost verbatim, but said just a bit
more clearly: it doesn't really matter how much you try?

Did Tanté scream for them both? *Maybe Tanté's already
screamed, maybe that's why she looked so free.*

The gallery is filled with different sounds, though: voices
eddying, swirling soft, loud, soft; staccato laughs; bottle clink-
ing on bottle; echoes raining down from the ceiling. Push
doesn't want to be here, in entangling sounds. But he stays for
Dave.

Dave. First one to call him Push. After-school programme
freshman year high school. One-thing-people-don't-know-
about-me exercise:

– My middle name is Pushkin. Alexander Pushkin Davis.

– Aah, parents with a love of Russian literature, the drama
teacher said. Push would always, everafter, think of that
teacher, Ms. Gonzales, when he heard the word sardonic.

– Damn, Pushkin? David. Yo, that's right there, boyee, that's it. I'm-a call you Push. He was never generic Alex or casual Al after. Even to his Africanist – the drama teacher was wrong, didn't know about Hannibal – even to his Africanist father.

Push finds Dave's entry near the slide show. Recognizes the triptych without seeing signature or plaque. A large panel in the centre, two smaller ones on either side. The left: Gandhi in Tianamen Square, tanks aimed at him, white dhoti, little glasses, placid smile and all. The right: Ben Franklin marching down Fifth Avenue flanked by leather boys and drag queens, trademark frock coat and knickers, grey pageboy – and his little wire-rimmed glasses. Push grins. Ben's flying a flag with rainbow colours; Roy G. Biv bows on the tail.

Gotta give the straight boy some credit for that one. Twisted with the paint brush. Push likes this about Dave, empathy and right-eousness and humour all mixed up.

Since high school. Hours in Mickey D's over fries and cokes: Push making observations about other customers and analysing events from school, Dave drawing wicked funny illustrations. Interrupted when they drifted: college away for Push, school in the city for Dave; Push's corporate job, Dave's artsy gigs. Gay, straight.

But one Friday night, years after – after high school and college, different jobs and new addresses – Push and Dave both ended up at the same restaurant on dates. And during the small talk, the how-ya-been-where-ya-living-how's-ya-mom's talk, Dave said, "First date right, I can tell. Dude's pretty nice looking, yo." Easy. A week later they catch a flick together, Big Mac's and fries afterward, and laughter. Now they talk like before. No, better than before, because now Push keeps no secrets.

– Better be early for my show tomorrow. Dave on the phone last night.

– Tomorrow? Damn, I thought it was. . . ain't it next. . .

–Yeah, yeah, you got mad jokes. But for real, my shit's gon' trip you out.

– Well you only been working on it for, what? Six months. It gotta trip somebody out.

– Just get your face in the place, Push.

– No doubt, check the mystery masterpiece.

The middle panel of the triptych – half as tall again as the others, twice as wide – is a Last Supper. In the centre, the Jesus spot, Huey Newton, dressed in full Panther regalia – black turtleneck, beret, gun-belt draped over his shoulder like a desert robe. Working down the table Push recognizes Stokely Carmichael (fist raised), Eldridge Cleaver (leather jacket, black shades), H. Rap Brown, Seale.

– So, I paint Stokely correct? Got your homie down right?

– It's a'ight," Push says without looking away from the canvas.

– Damn, that's all you got for a brother's blood, sweat and tears?

– Radical man. Push turns grinning. He 'hood-hugs Dave, brushing shoulders, right hand thumping his friend's back. You laid it down right, Radical with a capital 'R'.

– Yes! And how 'bout Ben?

– Funny as hell and. . . seriously solid. Push knows that Dave isn't just making small talk, that Dave really cares about what Push thinks of his work, his choices.

– And so why you givin' my boy Kûkai a hard time? Dave changes gears.

– Yo...

– Acting like you ain't who he think you are? Dave almost says this with a straight face, but cracks up into a laugh.

– Ain't funny, Push says, though he's laughing too.

Dave's been mostly in on this "joke" from the beginning, back when it started – harmless, random But Push's laugh now is mostly reflex, a conditioned reply to Dave's.

Six months ago Push dipped into a bodega for a bottle of water and the Middle Eastern guy behind the counter acknowledged him as a fellow Mohammedan: "Asalaam alaikum." Push paid and left and didn't give it a thought until days later. On Atlantic Avenue, a stout, old man crossed his path, dark parka over beige tunic, matching kufi on his head. The man stared directly at Push, his beard a surprise mirror. Again the greeting: Asalaam Alaikum. That time Push managed, "Alaikum Asalaam."

Push called Dave with the story.

– Yo, this is beautiful, now you can hail yellow cabs. Dave framed the mix-ups in humour. Hell, they might even bring your black ass 'cross the bridge to Brooklyn.

– Yeah? Let's test that theory 'bout eleven o'clock on a rainy Saturday night.

– Son, I'm-a buy you a little knit kufi to keep in your pocket. Throw that boy on your head – you be good to go.

That's how it began, Phase One.

As Push's beard grew in, creeping nappy up his cheeks, the sidewalk ID's shifted: "Lemme get a light, Dread." "Rasta man, buy some incense." On Fulton Street, ancient men in Clark's boots and red-and-green tams touched their hearts and nodded at Push, his own hair growing bushy under a knit cap.

But the fun left with the end of Phase One, months ago.
Phase Two was no game.

– Really ain't funny, Push says to David, now. So, who's he
think I am anyway?

– Kûkai loves your work, baby.

– Dude's into COBOL programmes, huh? *Everyone loves a
programmer, I know. COBOL = cold balls.*

– I ain't know 'bout all that, but likes your art though.
What'd he say? Yeah, he 'vibes with your message'.

– Nice, and what's my message?

– Thinks you Bill Abram, this real talented cat. And Iya, the
beautiful sister with the braids, thinks so too. Dave points out
the chick who asked Push if he was a painter.

– Please. And I bet this Abram guy is some kind of nut.

– Not a nut. . . kinda grumpy, definitely not a people
person. But guy's got some clout in the art game. Know what?
You sorta do look like him, my brother.

– You know what, if this wasn't your show, you know I'd
be outta here, right?

– Hell, wasn't my show, your ass'd still be hiding out in
your crib, watching TV.

– Believe that, Push says.

And that's the thing: he's not here, not staying here, because
Dave's just his friend. Dave's been an anchor, past few months.
Months when Push was drifting through life, unmoored from
the religions of God, money and love. *Throw out the life line,
somebody's drifting ah-wa-aa-ay.* With not much left to hang on
to, there was Dave. Frienship unwavering. Dave there.

– David, my dear, David, you're needed. Ghini's voice
floats from behind Push. She's Dave's agent. Calls him 'my

dear' and makes it sound like hip new slang. Hello Push. Good
to see you here.

– Ghini, how're you doin'?

– Beautiful. She's wearing a purple dress, cut West African
style, displaying her hips; her salt-and-pepper locks woven
into a basket on her head.

– I agree, Push says, forcing a smile. You look beautiful.
She gently touches his elbow.

– Got to steal our star for a minute though. David, they're
going to do a group photograph.

– A'ight I'm off. Dave hums *High-ho, High-ho* as he walks
away.

– Say cheese, Push calls after him.

Ghini leads Push in a conversation about the exhibit:
Dave's work, his talent, the industry big-wigs in the spot, and
her plans for his career. The topics are unfamiliar to the
computer programmer, but Push hangs tough. Push and
Ghini only talked this much once before – a birthday party
that fell in the middle of a wicked Nor'easter; only a half
dozen people showed. That conversation, with Ghini riffing
on "artistic passion" and "the power of the universe", karma
and ancestors – the philosophy that she lives by – was as
foreign to Push as a snowman in Trinidad. This room
tonight is warmer, noisier than the Raccoon Lounge was that
snowy night, but Push and Ghini, both good at carving space,
talk almost alone in the crowd.

– Push, have you ever thought about being a teacher?

– A teacher? *Hell, why not. Can't be a painter. Not a lover, or
a fighter.*

– Crazy question I know. But I see in you the disposition for teaching, for imparting knowledge. Ghini's eyes peer over her half-moon glasses, direct.

– Thanks, I guess.

– Oh! You don't know, I worked in the New York school system for years and years.

– Yeah? *Now, that makes sense. I can see you as a teacher.*

– Well I was a teacher, and a counsellor and a trainer too. And I consider myself a teacher, still.

– Right, Push nods.

– I worked with an Angolan man some years ago. His name was Gabriel De Terra. Such a handsome man, he had this deep voice, Ghini chuckling, bright. Push, watching her – he sees her "see" the man. A voice that could calm you, or could stop you in your tracks. But Gabby, I called him Gabby, had the most beautiful spirit – how can I say this – oh my! You could almost see it around him. We were good friends, you know.

In their space, the room retreats to ambient light and sound: flashbulbs strobe distant and irregular; shoes clickclack the concrete floor. Ghini's eyes grow big – large dark pupils, wide not-quite-white whites, lids shadowed, hollows deep. *Ghini's beautiful. So sure. So happy.*

– Well Push, I'll never forget this. One morning over coffee Gabby said to me, 'I won't be around much longer'. He was a young man, younger than me. He said, 'but, one day there'll be somebody who reminds you of me'. I could not imagine what he meant – that day. 'Not someone who just looks like me or talks like me, but an energy,' he said.

This is a story. Just conversation.

– Well Gabby didn't live more than three months after that. And now, all this time later, here we are, Push.

Ghini holds his elbow again, and locks his eyes in hers. Words hang in the air. *Tell me I ain't supposed to trip over this, tell me this.* Because Push is the "somebody" that Ghini had been told to expect. He listens, flattered and sympathetic. And bothered by it all. *This here tonight ain't nothing but some damned phase three.*

Phase One had been amusing, even adventurous. Monday an Arab, Tuesday a Rastafarian. Push like a kid in different carnival masks.

Phase Two came subtle. So quiet that he'd had to trace it back: dots here, dots there, a path that Push followed back to a February day. Walking home from Pathmark, balanced by plastic grocery bags in each hand, he'd picked his way over packed snow, trying to avoid ice patches and camouflaged dog shit. His mind slid from a long computer programme that he'd submitted overnight (*Did I set the sort keys right for that match?*), to the fastest meal he could make for dinner (*Maybe that can of soup, a turkey sandwich.*)

He didn't notice the woman until she was up on him, almost past him, close on his little strip of sidewalk. She gazed up, directly at him – eyes held on his face in a very un-New York way. But she wasn't a tourist, that lady with a puffy down coat and funky glasses, aluminium briefcase or something in one hand. Quick, a couple-a few seconds on Ashland Place, but strange enough to stick. Push remembered it afterwards – weeks afterwards, when he kept seeing that look again and again. Afterwards, when he'd label that look #1 in the connect-the-dots string.

Phase Two dragged on. Folks staring at him with some strange mosaic of emotions. For weeks, Push looked in random mirrored surfaces, trying to find what had caused the last stare. On rough days he double-checked, triple-checked his fly, inspected his nose for hanging boogers, his eyes for unwashed "sleep". On rare good days, his thoughts veered towards vanity, Push thinking, *Dude's checking me out.* Answers weren't ever that easy, though. The looks were overly familiar. Expectant. Intrusive. Always they'd lead Push to wonder, *What? What do these people want from me?*

Push didn't talk about Phase Two to anyone, even to Dave. Then, with the weather warming – new growth on trees, sap rising – Dave sensed a change in Push, made a big deal about Push isolating himself too much, needing some company. Forced him to hang out. So they did the familiar – pizza in The Village, walking on Broadway afterwards, checking out street vendors from Benin and Bhutan and the Bronx.

– Yo, yo! Dave said, nudging Push's shoulder near Prince Street.

A middle-aged woman with the perfect bob had just breezed through the doors of a gourmet deli and almost lost her footing as she looked over at Push. Stylish boxes dangled from her hands, and her lips went slack then tight to a smile – quick, from surprised to happy. Her eyes stayed on Push.

– Yo, who's that woman, Push? You know her?

– No, that's. . .

– Damn boy, she almost tripped over her own feet. Dave laughing, amazed. She was looking at you like. . . like. . . man, I don't even know. That's funny as hell.

– A riot, Push said.

And right there, Phase Two felt more real the moment Dave saw it. Push felt better and worse in an instant. Better to know that he wasn't imagining it all, worse 'cause he didn't know what "it all" was.

Push didn't try to explain the difference between Phase One and Phase Two to Dave. But there was a difference. It was one thing for someone to assume that he was a Muslim or Rasta, make an assumption, generalize. It was something else for strangers to stare at him, force themselves into his space.

Tonight, here was Phase Three. *One plus two. Commutative principle*. People thought he was someone else. Specific. Forced themselves into his space, and, they had expectations of him – because of who they'd decided he was. *Does not compute, Will Rogers.*

Bad enough with family who wanted him to be straight, get married, make babies. Men in clubs and bars who expected him to be thuggish, boyfriends who wanted a fixed sex role. A boss who wanted a drone, a quiet cog. Bad enough even with Dave wanting him to be happy. Happy. But now strangers wanted him to be this one and that, be Bill Abram, be Gabby De Terra. Be what? *Can I just be Push, just be*?

The real Tanté Tilda knew who she was when she took four children and left the man who fed and clothed them, the man who also beat her at whim. Stokely had to know his true self, regardless of whether they called him Stokely Carmichael or Kwame Touré, know deep in his spirit when he called for "Black Power". And don't you have to know who you are to stand in front of armed tanks? Don't you have to know when you march to the sea to mine un-taxed salt, fight the great British Empire? Did Push know once? Know spirit? Could he even remember Push-spirit, without the running, the hiding?

– Oh dear, I promised to chat with those folks. Collectors. Ghini winks as she walks away, none too soon. But I'm not done with you yet.

Push closes both eyes for a while, absurdly hoping that the gallery will be gone when he reopens them. But it's still there, all of it. So he goes off in search of the bathroom. Peeing – less to relieve his bladder than to relieve his mind. After, he stands at the sink, water running. He stares into the cheap mirror, between scratchy clouds, at Push. Beard, eyes, nose, lips yes. But Push. He splashes water on his face. Changes it from warm to cold. Splashes. Cold to hot. Splashes. *Splish-splash. Where's Tom Hanks when you need him?*

Truth is Push and Dave did stay in touch after high school. Until freshman year college, winter break. Dave dragged him to a party that night. Showed off his new friends. Artsy, straight. Everyone knew everyone else it seemed. Push might have been really mad at Dave that night for the first time. Pictured himself taking the subway back alone. Just leaving.

He walks out of the bathroom. Scans. Path from where he stands to the exit. Obstacles – loud, irregular but unavoidable blocks, placed almost precisely. Clusters of people, undecipherable sculpture, the makeshift bar. Ghini, Iya, Kûkai. Photographers, projectors. Push can almost laugh. Separate, none of the obstacles is even noticeable, worth mentioning. But the combination? *Combinations – that's how boxers get knocked down*. Huge strong men fall to the canvas from a one-two punch, so why not Push? *One, two.*

And it's the combination of life – the misidentifications, the expectations, the disappointments – the combinations that make Push want to run to the door. But he's ringed in. As he stands, one man from the crowd starts walking right at him. The man is holding a video camera, staring not directly at Push, but down into the viewfinder. Moving directly toward him. The cameraman isn't panning the room or recording the background art, just moving nearer and nearer.

– Mr. Abram, how 'bout some thoughts on the show.

Push shakes his head. He wants to say something, but the words in his mind don't add up. *I'm not Bill Abram, I'm Gabby.*

The camera close, Push shakes his head faster, back and forth – childlike.

– Just a few words, Mr. Abram.

– No, all Push can muster. And the "no" doesn't even sound like his own voice and isn't loud enough to travel past his own ears.

– Yes. An arm wraps around Push's shoulder from the left. Dave grinning. Yes, 'Mr. Abram', a few words.

– Ooh, don't move. Let me get this shot, Iya sings. She's moving in from the right with a digital camera.

– Sure thing. How's this? Dave pulls Push so that their shoulders touch.

– Marvellous shot, Ghini's voice comes from the back. Great artist stands with great teacher!

– No, Push says.

But he knows that no one's heard him. Not cameraman, not Iya, not Ghini. Most of all not Dave who is so close. *So close and so far.* He came for Dave, the one who understood. Dave who's humour could light, once. Dave with passion that inspired. But now the closer Dave moves – hugging, laughing – the further Push feels from his last link. Now the humour hits. *Last straw. House of straw. Huff and puff. Blow me down.*

– No! Now loud enough to make them stop. It makes them all stop – those who have formed ropes around him and the others through the gallery.

Push flings Dave's arm away and this time he does leave. Now the clarity is there. Interpretation: Dave is symbol of all that Push does not know how to do. *No!* Through the crowd, past the images, right past the rusty gate.

A thin breeze greets Push in the Brooklyn night – cooler than earlier. Red Hook buildings carve skeletons against an indigo sky, like dinosaur exhibits in a museum after hours. Telephone wires sag from wood poles, recalling yesterdays. Uneven cobblestone patches poke history through asphalt streets.

Rushing, the gallery behind, Push feels its aura about him yet. The flash bulbs, tracking him like Iya's eyes, and posing him like Kûkai, fixing him like Ghini. All of it seeping into him. Push – like film overexposed, camera opened, darkroom door thrown wide. Push runs west. Towards the water.

What to do? What? Maybe he could just shave. Shave and turn back time. But maybe that would make it all worse – the exposure, the wanting, the demands from random people, from some unknown force, from life. The fact is that Phase Three has come so definite, so hard tonight that Push knows he couldn't live with it. Damn sure couldn't make it to whatever a Phase Four might be. Maybe it ain't about the external. Maybe something's got to change inside. Could he just give them each, give them all, what they wanted? Or force them to deal with what he wanted? But Push has stopped wanting.

Thinking back, Push sees Phase One – false masks placed on him with complete assurance. Phase Two – invasions that left him confused, wondering. And tonight, this shift, this Phase Three. To Kûkai and Iya he is Bill Abram. To Ghinni he is Gabriel De Terra. To Dave it's a joke. And to him it is too much. All too much. One, Two, Three – Push must do something. *No. It's not them. No. It's me. No. There is no me. No.*

Running though the spotty dark, Push is all arms and legs. His elbows, wrists, knees bend to carve a fluid space of then and now. His heart pumps Shango rhythm, blood coursing to match a chorus of drums in his head. *Rumdrum, rumdrum, no.* At the water's edge Push's scream fills the night. Raw sound fills each unseen nook in the dark. Naked noise reaches far, pierces high. Here is the scream that Push has stifled too long.

ACKNOWLEDGEMENTS

Immeasurable thanks for family who love me perfectly in my imperfection. Mummy, Daddy, Penny – I would pick you all if I had the chance to pick. Aunts, uncles, cousins, nephew, niece. Grandmothers – my cup runneth over.

Friends brave enough to act like family: Aatom – always. Alvin. Ernest, Cecelia, Ken, Peter, Ronald. Cheryl. Darell. Michael and Nancy. Leona and Kathy.

Creative family, for reading, listening, inspiring, encouraging: Yolaine, Nhojj, Colin, Cheryl, Pamela; Nkiru/Open Spaces, especially Yogini and Natasha. Vona Voices; Louder Arts. Caribbean Cultural Theatre. CSV, who introduced me to the form. Jacqueline, who opened the gate.

ABOUT THE AUTHOR

Anton Nimblett is a Trinidadian living and writing in Brooklyn. He has been published in Calabash: A Journal of Caribbean Arts and Letters and in African Voices. His fiction is included in the anthology *Our Caribbean: A Gathering of Lesbian and Gay Writing From the Antilles*, edited by Thomas Glave.

David Dabydeen
Our Lady of Demerara
ISBN: 9781845230692; pp. 288; August 2008; £9.99

The ritual murder of a mysterious Indian girl and the flight of seedy drama critic from his haunts in the back street of Coventry to the Guyana wilds to find out more about the fragmented journals of an Irish missionary in Demerara are brought together in a hugely imaginative exploration of spiritual malaise and redemption.

Brenda Flanagan
Allah in the Islands
ISBN: 9781845231064; pp. 216, August 2009; £8.99

When Beatrice Salandy, first met in Flanagan's novel, *You Alone are Dancing*, is acquitted in a trial that divides the sympathies of the people of Santabella between rulers and ruled, she attracts the attention of the Haji, the charismatic leader of a radical Muslim group. Against her judgement, Beatrice is drawn into his orbit.

Curdella Forbes
A Permanent Freedom
ISBN: 9781845230616; pp. 210; July 2008, £8.99

Crossing the space between the novel and short fiction, this collection weaves nine individual stories about love, sex, death and migration into a single compelling narrative that seizes the imagination with all the courage, integrity and folly of which the human spirit is capable.

Earl Long
Leaves in a River
ISBN: 9781845230081; pp. 208; November 2008; £8.99

What brings Charlo Pardie, a peasant farmer on an island not unlike St. Lucia, on the edge of old age, to leave his wife, family and land and take himself to the house of Ismene L'Aube, known to all as a prostitute? And what, three years later, takes him home again?

Geoffrey Philp
Who's Your Daddy? and Other Stories
ISBN: 9781845230777; pp. 160; April 2009; £7.99

Whether set in the Jamaican past or the Miami present, whether dealing with sexual errantry, skin-shade and culture wars, with manifestations of the uncanny, or with teenage homophobia, Geoffrey Philp's second collection confirms his status as a born storyteller.

Patricia Powell
The Fullness of Everything
ISBN: 9781845231132; pp. 240; May 2009; £8.99

When Winston receives a telegram informing him of his father's imminent death, his return to Jamaica is very reluctant. 25 years in the USA without contact with his family has allowed mutual resentments to mature. Told through the perspectives of Winston and his estranged brother, the novel explores the power of past hurts and the possibilities of transcending them.

Raymond Ramcharitar
The Island Quintet
ISBN: 9781845230753; pp. 232; June 2009; £8.99

In these sometimes seamy, often darkly comic and bracingly satirical stories, Ramcharitar reveals Trinidad as a globalised island with permeable borders, frequent birds of passage and outposts in New York and London. His characters scramble for survival, fame and fortune in an island struggling to come to terms with both its history and its present.

Ed. Courttia Newland & Monique Roffey
Tell-Tales Four: The Global Village
ISBN: 9781845230791; pp. 212; March 2009; £8.99

With contributions from Olive Senior, Matt Thorne, Sophie Woolley, Adam Thorpe, Catherine Smith and twenty others, this collection of stories from the UK-based Tell-Tales literary collective touches on love, sex, death, war, global warming, immigration and crime in sometimes dark and sometimes funny ways.

CARIBBEAN MODERN CLASSICS

Jan R. Carew   *Spring 2009 titles*
Black Midas
Introduction: Kwame Dawes
ISBN: 9781845230951; pp. 272; 23 May 2009; £8.99

This is the bawdy, Eldoradean epic of the legendary 'Ocean Shark', first published in 1958, who makes and loses fortunes as a pork-knocker in the gold and diamond fields of Guyana, discovering that there are sharks with far sharper teeth in the city.

Jan R. Carew
The Wild Coast
Introduction: Jeremy Poynting
ISBN: 9781845231101; pp. 240; 23 May 2009; £8.99

A sickly city child is sent away to the remote Berbice village of Tarlogie. Here he must find himself, make sense of Guyana's diverse cultural inheritances and come to terms with a wild nature disturbingly red in tooth and claw.

Neville Dawes
The Last Enchantment
Introduction: Kwame Dawes
ISBN: 9781845231170; pp. 332; 27 April 2009; £9.99

This penetrating and often satirical exploration of the search for self in a world divided by colour and class is set in the context of the radical hopes of Jamaican nationalist politics in the early 1950s. First published in 1960, the novel asks many pertinent questions about the Jamaica of today.

Wilson Harris
Heartland
Introduction: David Dabydeen
ISBN: 9781845230968; pp. 104; 23 May 2009; £7.99

First published in 1964, this visionary novel tracks a man's psychic disintegration in the aloneness of the forests of the Guyanese interior, making a powerful ecological statement about man's place in the 'invisible chain of being', in which nature is a no less active presence.

Edgar Mittelholzer
Corentyne Thunder
Introduction: Juanita Cox
ISBN: 9781845231118; pp. 242; 27 April 2009; £8.99

This pioneering work of West Indian fiction is not merely an acute portrayal of the rural Indo-Guyanese world, but a work of literary ambition that creates a symphonic relationship between its characters and the vast openness of the Corentyne coast.

Andrew Salkey
Escape to an Autumn Pavement
Introduction: Thomas Glave
ISBN: 9781845230982; pp. 220; 23 May 2009; £8.99

This brave and remarkable novel, set in London at the end of the 1950s catches its 'brown' Jamaican narrator on the cusp between black and white, between exiled Jamaican and an incipent black Londoner, and between heterosexual and homosexual desires.

Denis Williams
Other Leopards
Introduction: Victor Ramraj
ISBN: 9781845230678; pp. 216; 23 May 2009; £8.99

Lionel Froad is a Guyanese working on an archeological survey in the mythical Jokhara in the horn of Africa. There he hopes to rediscover the self he calls 'Lobo', his alter ego from 'ancestral times', which he thinks slumbers behind his cultivated mask. Denis Williams

The Third Temptation
Introduction: Victor Ramraj
ISBN: 9781845231163; pp. 108; 23 May 2009; £7.99

A young man is killed in a traffic accident at a Welsh seaside resort. Around this incident, Williams, drawing inspiration from the *Nouveau Roman*, creates a reality that is both rich and problematic. Whilst he brings to the novel a Caribbean eye, Williams refuses any restrictive boundaries for Caribbean fiction.